"What kind of woman am I?"

"Soft, sweet smelling." Matthew ran a finger under her lacy blouse collar. "Pink cotton candy, the lady on the chocolate box, the kind a boy dreams about. Not a woman for shoveling out stalls or facing over the breakfast table, but a woman for loving on warm summer nights."

Charlotte dropped her eyes to hide a flash of anger.

"That's very pretty talk, Matthew." The open V of his faded blue shirt exposed skin tanned to golden brown. "But you make me sound rather insubstantial."

"Dream ladies usually are." He tipped up her chin. "Although I don't remember any of the ladies of my boyhood dreams having freckles. Maybe I didn't look closely enough." Shoving back his hat, he lowered his head.

Dear Reader,

For many years I dreamed of being a writer. One day
my husband wisely pointed out I needed to quit
dreaming about writing and do it. So I did, but the
dream came first. Now I'm lucky because I can dream
in print.

My books are pure flights of fancy, the characters
wholly imaginary, and yet, all my stories draw in some
way from my own experiences. Charlotte grew out of
my love of old linens and lace. I knew she would
appreciate the care and love that goes into the creating
and preserving of such family treasures.

Charlotte personifies the strength and gentleness that
combine in every woman. Naturally I wanted the right
man for her. Being a firm believer in the old adage
"Opposites attract", I wasn't surprised when a rugged
rancher rode up. Maybe at first Matthew and Charlotte
weren't each other's idea of a "dream come true", but I
quickly set them straight. Well, not too quickly. I had
some fun along the way and I hope you do, too.

Jeanne Allan

Charlotte's Cowboy
Jeanne Allan

Harlequin Books

TORONTO • NEW YORK • LONDON
AMSTERDAM • PARIS • SYDNEY • HAMBURG
STOCKHOLM • ATHENS • TOKYO • MILAN
MADRID • WARSAW • BUDAPEST • AUCKLAND

ISBN 0-373-03384-2

CHARLOTTE'S COWBOY

First North American Publication 1995.

Copyright © 1995 by Jeanne Allan.

Printed in U.S.A.

CHAPTER ONE

THE cowboy was back. Charlotte watched him from beneath lowered lashes. This was the third time he'd approached Romance and Old Lace. He had yet to enter the store. The first time he'd stood outside looking through the plate-glass window. She'd been showing a customer the old embroidered pillowcases displayed in the window and had felt his eyes on her. He was a stranger, tall with hard-edged good looks. Something about him made her nervous, and she'd been happy when he'd walked away. The second time, Charlotte had looked up to see him studying her through the store's open doorway. There was a frown on his face, and when their gazes met, she thought he intended to speak to her, but a prospective bride with her mother in tow had swept past him into the store. Charlotte greeted them, and when she'd looked at the doorway, he was gone.

Now he was back and staring at the contents of the show window. While Charlotte was immensely pleased with the romantic all-white vignettes she'd contrived from odd bits of china, old linens and flower-bedecked hats, she found it difficult to believe the display was holding this particular man in thrall. He was obviously waiting for her current customers to leave.

On the other side of the small store, two women about Charlotte's age discussed their husbands' inability to wax romantic and the relative merits of several finely tucked lawn nightgowns. Charlotte had shown them all she had in their sizes and moved away while they made up their minds.

She was free to speculate on the man's recurrent appearances. Straightening a fragrant display of soap that earlier customers had disturbed, Charlotte considered the possibility that the man was a husband, determined to purchase something of an intimate nature for his wife, but shy about it. Somehow he didn't seem the shy type. He looked more the type to wade right in, the devil with the consequences. Charlotte moved to a table heaped with silk scarves. The colors glowed under the store lights; the fabric glided smoothly over her skin. Another stealthy peek through lowered lashes located him still on the other side of the showcase window.

He was beginning to irritate her. If he was a customer, he should come in. Except she knew he wasn't a customer. He was one of those darned throwbacks from another century. Men who still played with cows and horses and thought rules of polite behavior were for other people. Men who grabbed what they wanted and rode off into the sunset when they didn't want it any more. Men who were hard and unforgiving, whose emotions were as dried up as the dusty pastures they lorded over. Charlotte knew all about those kind of men, and the cowboy was definitely one of them. From the wide brim of a dark felt hat down to dusty boots, all six feet plus of him absolutely reeked of self-assurance. Totally absorbed in his own thoughts, he was oblivious to the curious and flirtatious looks passing women flashed at him. Oblivious or accustomed to women reacting to the sheer masculinity of rugged good looks and a powerful frame. Whatever else he was, he was all male, with long legs encased in tight jeans that accentuated strong-looking, muscular thighs. His kind was always disgustingly good-looking. It came with the territory. Rearranging floral china sugar bowls, Charlotte wondered what color his eyes were. Not that she gave a hoot. Blue-eyed, green-eyed or brown-eyed, cowboys left her cold.

Movement outside the store told her she wouldn't have to worry about this particular cowboy. She watched him stride away down the mall, the rigid set of his wide shoulders registering annoyance. Charlotte felt like shouting after him she couldn't be expected to eject everyone from the store to suit his convenience. All that sitting on a horse looking down must make a man think he was above the rest of the world. What a shame to waste rugged good looks on a man who doubtless possessed a brain as bovine as the cows he normally associated with.

"I'll take this one." The dark-haired woman smiled and held up a Victorian-style gown. Charlotte quit speculating about the stranger and turned her attention to business.

The cowboy returned a few minutes before closing time, once again scanning the shop's interior through the display window. Framed by the unabashedly romantic showcase, the contrast of rugged male and delicate linens forcibly struck Charlotte. This man would never consider buying a froth of lace for his wife to wear. Good old-fashioned flannel, that's what he'd select. The cowboy walked into the store, his nostrils flaring in mild distaste at the exotic-smelling scent of potpourri perfuming the air, all the while his gaze intent on her. He'd removed his hat, and a tanned face and sun-bleached highlights in chestnut brown hair confirmed he spent long hours outdoors. A real cowboy, she thought, not a drugstore cowboy dressed up to impress women.

Apprehension flooded over her. Please let him be a customer. She cleared her throat. "May I help you?"

"You're Charlotte Darnelle." It was not a question.

"Yes." Her plea was not going to be answered.

"Your grandfather sent me." There was a cool challenge in the statement.

"Is your name Michael?"

His brows drew together at the faint tinge of mockery in her voice. "It's Matthew. Matthew Thorneton. Your grandfather—"

"Grandpa Darnelle died two years ago." She refused to let him finish. "That's why I thought your name must be Michael. As in the archangel."

"You had two grandfathers. Your other—"

"I had one grandfather. His name was Richard Darnelle." Charlotte walked to the doorway. "We close early on Sundays."

His frown deepened. "I don't think you understand, Ms. Darnelle."

"It's not my understanding that's deficient." She pulled the metal gate used to close the store halfway across the opening. "Goodbye." When he didn't move but stood looking at her, frustration riding his face, she added pointedly, "I can call mall security." The man moved slowly through the doorway. On the other side of the gate he stopped to watch her fasten the chain. She ignored him, willing him to go away. Looking past the lock she saw his scarred and dirty boots remain adamantly within her field of vision.

"I didn't choose to come to Denver. I'm here for your benefit." His voice was deep. And riddled with irritation. He was obviously a man who wasn't used to being crossed. He was also an itch that wouldn't go away.

Charlotte scratched. "The only thing you can do to benefit me is disappear."

"You remind me of Charlie Gannen. Your other grandfather." His voice underlined the last two words.

Anger brought her head up. "That's not a compliment."

"It wasn't meant to be. He could be a real son of...a real pain."

Charlotte turned away. This cowboy wasn't telling her anything she didn't know. Ignoring him, she walked over to the counter and continued her closing-up routine. When she looked again, the man was gone. She threw her pen on the countertop. So that was Matthew Thorneton. She should have guessed who he was the minute she saw him. He was as overbearing and self-righteous in person as he'd been in his letters. The first letter had been a stiffly worded appraisal of Charles Gannen's health, accompanied by the suggestion, worded more as a command, that, as Charles Gannen's only grandchild, she come visit the ailing old man. She'd scrawled "Not interested" across the page and sent it back. The second letter had been even less diplomatic. More sermon than invitation, it had taken her to task for her refusal to come. Claiming a dying man needed his family, even if he wouldn't admit Charlotte was his granddaughter. Telling her she owed it to her dead father's memory to forgive his father. Chick Gannen was her biological father, but that didn't mean she owed him anything. By what right did the cowboy judge her behavior? Calling her cold and unfeeling, derelict in family responsibilities. His third letter she'd sent back unopened.

She had opened the short letter from some lawyer telling her Charles Gannen was dead. The letter had been carefully worded to avoid any suggestion that Charlotte was the old man's granddaughter. Even in death Charles Gannen had refused to acknowledge their relationship. Was that why the cowboy was here? The old man's hand reaching from the grave to warn her away from what had been his? Her upper lip curled derisively. As if she'd rush to Durango for her share of the spoils. Spoils. If ever there was an appropriate word. Anything left behind by Charles Gannen was bound to be tainted. She wanted none of it. Just as she wanted none of a tall, hulking cowboy. No matter how golden-brown his eyes were.

The golden-brown eyes were hidden behind sunglasses when Charlotte walked up to her car. She didn't ask how he knew which car was hers. A couple of smiles, a couple of lies... The fact he'd been able to ingratiate himself with one of the other shop owners in the mall didn't mean she had to listen to anything the big hunk of muscle leaning against her front fender had to say. Stepping precisely around his crossed boots, she pulled her car keys from her purse. "If you make one move to touch me, I'll scream."

"I'll just follow you home," he said conversationally. "You might as well listen to me now, and save us both trouble."

Follow her home. Home, where she lived with her mother, her grandmother Darnelle and her great-aunt Faye. The same home her mother had taken refuge in after finding herself pregnant, unmarried and grieving the loss of her only love in Vietnam. Charlotte hesitated, her fingers gripping a key. In the parking lot three magpies squabbled over spilled popcorn. There was no point in trying to lose him in traffic. He knew her address. "I told you before. Charles Gannen is, was, nothing to me."

"He left no descendants. Except you."

"Did he say so before he died? Did he leave anything written down naming me his granddaughter?"

The man hesitated. "No."

It shouldn't have hurt, but it did. And he knew it. She'd heard the tinge of pity in his voice. Her voice flattened. "I wasn't interested in him when he was alive and I'm not interested in him now he's dead." She stuck the key in the car door. "And don't give me any of that drivel you put in your letter about me being his only remaining family. He never considered me so. You admitted it yourself in the letter."

"Toward the end, I think he regretted never meeting you. He probably would have asked for you, but he ran out of time." His lips curved slightly. "It must have come as a hell of a shock to him. Finding out he couldn't have his own way for once." His mouth firmed. "I told you in the letter I thought he was willing to acknowledge you if you'd make the first move."

The air smelled of ozone, and puddles dotted the asphalt. A spring shower must have passed through earlier. Inches from her feet a dark rainbow glittered greasily across the surface of an oil slick. Charlotte shivered as a sudden breeze cooled her bare arms. She should have put on her jacket. Her fingers tightened around the cold metal door handle. "I'm not a good enough actress to play the big reconciliation scene."

"You really hated him, didn't you?"

"You have to know someone to hate him. I didn't care about Charles Gannen one way or the other." She slid behind the wheel. "Goodbye, Mr. Thorneton."

He grabbed the edge of the door, holding it open. "Don't you want to know why I'm here?"

"No."

"Charlie Gannen sent me."

"He's dead."

"He left a letter with instructions."

"I can imagine. One last curse. One last disavowal of my existence. One last proclamation that his son Chick couldn't possibly have fathered me." She reached for the door. "You and your instructions can turn around and go right back to Durango."

"I'll be happy to. If you'll ever shut up long enough for me to explain why I'm here."

"You don't seem to understand, Mr. Thorneton. I don't care why you are in Denver. Charles Gannen swore before I was born he'd never have anything to do with me, and whatever else can be said of Charles Gannen, he was a man of his word. It would take more than death for him to break his vow."

"He left you his ranch."

Charlotte knew her mouth must be hanging open, but she'd lost control over her face muscles. A bubble of laughter rose in her throat. She swallowed hard. "You must be joking."

"It's no joke. His entire estate goes to you."

It had to be a joke. It was too improbable. After twenty-four years... She tapped the center of the steering wheel, her mind groping with the astonishing news. More to give her time than because she cared, she asked, "What did he leave?"

"I thought you weren't interested."

"I'm curious, is all."

"Funny how the thought of inheriting a fortune can stir up a person's curiosity."

"Did he leave a fortune?"

"Charlie was comfortable."

"What does that mean?"

"No gold mines or oil wells." Behind the tinted glasses, Matthew Thorneton's face was unreadable. "A house, some outbuildings, a few acres. This and that. It's all laid out in the will."

She stared at him. There was something queer about all this. Matthew Thorneton wasn't telling the truth. Not the whole truth. It was in his voice. "He died six months ago."

"If you filed any claim on Charlie Gannen's estate within six months of the time the lawyer notified you of his death, the estate was to go elsewhere." He answered the unasked question in a monotone.

Charlotte burst out laughing. Even dead, the old man managed to insult her. Matthew Thorneton couldn't have looked more astonished if she'd grown wings and a tail. Laughing helplessly, she stuck her key in the ignition. The car engine roared to life. "You can take Charles Gannen's estate and stuff it in his coffin." She wrestled away the car door and slammed it shut. Her eyes gritty, she tromped too hard on the accelerator, and her tires momentarily spun against some loose gravel before grabbing hold. It wasn't her fault the idiot cowboy had chosen to stand so close to a puddle of rainwater.

Traffic whizzed past on the busy streets. Pedestrians strolled the pathways through Washington Park. To the west the sun dipped below the rim of the Rocky Mountains. A typical late May Sunday afternoon in Denver, Colorado. Charlotte laughed again. An insult from the grave. It was too ludicrous for words. Her laughter was too high, too shrill, but laughter was her only defense. The idea of Charles Gannen believing she'd make some claim on him after death when she'd asked nothing of him while he was living... And then offering her his estate. Did he think she'd fall on his gravestone slobbering with gratitude? Did he think she didn't know how he'd treated her mother twenty-five years ago? Amusement fled. Poor Jewel. Pregnant, unwed and called a liar by the man who'd never be her father-in-law. Charles Gannen had adamantly refused to believe his precious son could have fathered a baby out of wedlock. Charlotte's knuckles whitened as she clung to the steering wheel. Maybe she should have gone to visit

Charles Gannen on his deathbed. She could have spit in the old man's eye.

The cowboy was too tall, or she would have spit in his eye. Splashing him with rainwater hardly did justice to her feelings. A reluctant smile curved her lips. The cowboy had a definite talent for swearing. His words had followed her halfway across the parking lot. She wondered how he'd become involved. Something about his squared-off jaw and arrogant stance said he was used to giving the orders. So why was he Charles Gannen's errand boy?

One look at the mud-splattered black pickup truck parked in front of her house and Charlotte knew she could ask him herself. Two long denim-clad legs unfurled from the pickup and a pair of worn boots were planted in the street. Charlotte debated with herself for less than a minute before marching over to the truck. "You delivered your message. Charles Gannen left me his estate. Thank you for telling me. Now go away."

He stood up. "You didn't let me finish."

She despised herself for taking a quick step back. It was just that he took up so much room. She flicked her ivory-colored skirt to one side in a pretense that her recoil was based on fastidiousness rather than uneasiness. "I was finished."

He followed her up the long sidewalk. "It's not quite that simple. There's a small condition."

"Of course there is." She kept walking. "I suppose I have to prove I'm Charles Gannen's granddaughter. Forget it. I couldn't if I wanted to."

"He said nothing about proving your parentage. I was to tell you, if you want the estate, you have to go live on his ranch for two weeks, said visit to begin within three months of my notifying you about the will and its condition."

"Fine. You've told me. Now get in your truck like a good little errand boy and go back to Durango." She sent a cool look over her shoulder. "Don't bother to air out the guest room. Because I won't be visiting."

"Don't you think you ought to discuss the matter with your mother?"

She stopped and turned. "Don't tell me he left her anything, because I wouldn't believe it."

"Charlie Gannen wasn't into forgiving or forgetting when someone crossed him. The letter specifically said you lose everything if she accompanies you to the ranch."

"Isn't it lucky I have no intention of going?"

"Aren't you interested in what happens to his estate if you don't come to Durango?"

"No."

"It goes to Connie Maywell." At her blank look, he added impatiently, "The woman your father was engaged to marry."

"I hope she enjoys it." Once again she headed up the walk.

He grabbed her arm and swung her about. "Charlie's first wife, your grandmother, Emily Gannen, died not too long after your father was killed in Vietnam. Charlie almost went crazy."

"Good for her. She was well rid of him." Pain shot through her arm as his fingers tightened.

"Charlie remarried about ten years ago. His second wife was good to him, putting up with his contrariness, nursing him during his last illness. You might even say she made him happy." A hint of anger flashed across his face. "Charlie didn't leave her a red cent."

"She can have my share. I don't want it."

"You don't have a share to give. Not until you stay at the ranch for two weeks. Then you can sell the ranch to me. The second Mrs. Gannen will be provided for."

"Forget it." She shook loose his hand and brushed imaginary dirt from her sleeve. "I'm not going to the ranch. As for his wife, she was a fool if she didn't know what he was like when she married him."

"You're like him. Stubborn as a mule."

"Name-calling won't get you anywhere. I long ago grew a thick skin in order to survive."

"We do feel sorry for ourselves, don't we? How much is it going to take to make little Charlotte feel better?"

She frowned in puzzlement. "How much what?"

"How much money to overcome your self-pity."

"If that's your idea of salesmanship, it stinks."

He stalked her up the walk. "I'm going to hound your footsteps until you agree to my proposition. All you have to do is take a two-week vacation on the ranch and it's yours. Then you sell it to me for fair market value."

"Why?" Charlotte spun around and eyed him suspiciously. "Why do you want something you described as just a house, some outbuildings, a few acres and this and that?"

"Charlie's second wife deserves more than a backhanded slap across the face."

"What's she to you?"

"She's—" he paused "—special to me."

"Why didn't she come do her own begging? Did she think you'd be more persuasive? That I'd be swept off my feet by some handsome hunk of brown-eyed cowboy?"

"It's happened before."

Red spots of anger rampaged across her vision. "If you mean my mother," she said furiously, "Chick Gannen's eyes were green." She whirled away.

"Wait." He stepped in front of her. "I'm sorry. I didn't mean... The handsome hunk bit threw me. I wasn't talking about— That is..."

"My mother and Chick Gannen. Go ahead. Say it. My mother fell for a handsome hunk of cowboy, and they slept together without benefit of wedding vows. Mrs. Charles Gannen no doubt thought it extremely clever to sic a cowboy on me. Like mother, like daughter." She stomped around him.

"She knew I was coming to Denver to see you." He kept pace with her. "She didn't know I was going to try to reach an agreement with you to buy the ranch."

"Then you won't have to report you failed, will you?"

He moved to stand between her and the front door. "Listen, Ms. Darnelle, you may as well accept that I'm not leaving Denver until you agree to visit your grandfather Gannen's ranch."

"Enjoy your stay because I'm not going to any ranch."

The door opened behind him, and Charlotte's mother peered around his large frame. "I thought I heard voices," Jewel said. "Why are you keeping your friend on the doorstep, Charlotte? Bring him in."

"He's not my friend and he's leaving."

The cowboy turned around and extended his hand. "Matthew Thorneton, Mrs....uh, that is, ma'am."

"Tricky, isn't it?" Charlotte asked. "Just exactly what is the proper way to address someone's mother when she's never been married?" She couldn't help the bitterness edging her voice.

Her small hand swallowed up by the larger masculine one, Jewel looked from Charlotte to the stranger. A bemused look on her face, she said softly, "It's nice to meet you, Mr. Thorneton. I'm Jewel Darnelle."

"Now I understand why Chick fell head over heels in love with you."

Charlotte wanted to slug him. Of all the dirty, low-down, conniving tricks. To remind her mother of the past. Not that her mother seemed to mind. Jewel absolutely glowed, clinging gratefully to the cowboy's hand as if he'd handed her a million dollars. As for him, the insincere, lying louse, he ought to be in Hollywood. The way his face softened and his brown eyes warmed up. Who was he kidding? He'd stoop to any level to get the estate for his special friend. She'd settle his hash. "Charles Gannen sent him, Mother."

Her mother's free hand fluttered slowly toward her throat. "Chick's father? Is that true, Mr. Thorneton? I thought, that is, Charlotte received a letter saying he was dead."

"Please. Call me Matt." His cool gaze held Charlotte's. "Charlie asked me to give a message to Charlotte."

"Not a message, an ultimatum. One I choose to ignore." Charlotte made the explanation for her mother, but the angry glare was aimed at the man blocking Charlotte's path.

Matthew Thorneton said to Jewel, "Charlie left everything to Charlotte on one condition. She inherits his estate if she spends two weeks on his ranch. It seems simple enough to me, but your daughter is being stubborn."

"Stubborn!" She ground her teeth together. "You're not telling all of it." Charlotte looked at her mother. "Apparently lack of relatives convinced Charles Gannen to accept the result of his son's fall from grace, but he's not about to forgive the evil woman who led him into sin. You were blatantly excluded from the command invitation." Renewed anger at the implied slur against her mother in Charles Gannen's will drove Charlotte headlong into speech meant to shock the old man's opportunistic errand boy. "Obviously you're a fallen woman who seduced Daddy's little boy, and Mr. Gannen was afraid if you stepped foot on his place, the very dirt would be contaminated.'' Her mother's white face immediately told Charlotte her arrows had wounded the wrong target.

"I think there's a better place to discuss this than on the front doorstep." Aunt Faye's crisp voice came from beyond the open door. "Come inside." The invitation from Charlotte's great-aunt, the younger sister of Charlotte's Grandpa Darnelle, was more of a directive.

As Jewel complied, Charlotte put a restraining hand on Matthew Thorneton's arm. "She didn't mean you."

"You're a real brat, aren't you?" Contemptuously he shook off her hand and followed Charlotte's mother inside.

Leaving Charlotte on the doorstep acknowledging she'd behaved badly. Not that she cared what he thought, but the one person she never could bear to hurt was her mother. Jewel had suffered enough.

It was inevitable that Charlotte's mother invited Matthew Thorneton to eat dinner with them, not from curiosity, but to offset her daughter's deplorable behavior. Charlotte covertly watched him as he easily conversed with the three women she loved best in the world. If he felt the slightest bit discomfited at finding himself the only male at the table, he hid it well. Obviously it would take more than a roomful of women or a shop full of lace and unmentionables to disturb this smug bastion of lazy male self-assurance.

Sunday was the only evening when everyone in the Darnelle family could sit down to dinner together, and by custom, it was an elegant meal. Candles flickered on the table, and overhead the electric chandelier was switched to low, a compromise her grandparents had reached over forty years ago and one Grandma Darnelle continued to honor. The soft lighting blessed the dining room, shielding from critical eyes water stains on the wallpaper and worn spots in the carpet. Charlotte looked with quiet pride at the mismatched silver, polished with the patina of age. The white tablecloth had been mended, a treasure from the past. She'd paid a quarter for it at a garage sale. Aunt Faye had unearthed the wineglasses at an estate sale, paying a rock-bottom price because there were only five left unbroken.

Charlotte loved Sunday dinners. Until tonight. She wanted to scream. To remind everyone why Matthew Thorneton was here. But she couldn't. Not at Sunday dinner with its unwritten rules of conduct. No arguing. No scolding. No unpleasantness. No problems for solving. The Sunday meal was reserved for best behaviors, interesting tidbits, amusing stories and the pleasure of being with those who loved you best. That pleasure didn't include the complacent toad sitting across the table from her.

An old gold-framed mirror hanging on the wall behind Matthew Thorneton reflected the back of his head, his dark hair thick and wavy, the ends barely curling under to brush against his collar. Sharing the mirror, Charlotte's image was a pale blob with ivory skin and pale red hair, her green eyes reduced to dark smudges in the dim light. At least her freckles weren't visible. Piling her wavy hair atop her head with long curls hanging down in front of her ears accentuated her long neck, making her head look like an apple on a stick, but customers expected her and Aunt Faye to match the ambiance of the shop, and the hairdo suited her old-fashioned shirtwaist with its high ruffled lace collar. Outwardly Charlotte was the picture of ladylike gentility.

Inwardly she seethed. She wanted to throw her plate at Matthew Thorneton's head. Followed by her wineglass. What was worse, he knew it and was laughing at her. She didn't know why she was so sure of that because he seldom looked at her and not once had he directed a comment her way. His presence shrunk the dining room, the dark floral walls closing in on her.

It was a relief when Aunt Faye finally suggested they move with their coffee to the living room. In the brightly lit larger room with its easy, faded furniture and abundance of family photographs, Charlotte could lay the outrageous proposition before her family. Matthew Thorneton would be out the front door before he had time to drain his cup.

Turning to her mother, he stole the initiative from Charlotte. "It's no secret how Charlie could hang on to a grievance. Considering he and Charlotte never met, I can't get over how much like him she is. I'd blame the red hair, but her father had red hair, and you know how easy going Chick Gannen was. And Charlie Gannen was no redhead."

"My hair is strawberry-blond, not red. You can insult me all you want, but I'm not going to that ranch."

"As I understand it, you have to go to inherit," Aunt Faye said.

"I don't want anything of his."

Matthew Thorneton turned to Charlotte's great-aunt. "Once Charlotte inherits, I'll be glad to buy the ranch from her, but she can't inherit without fulfilling the terms of the will."

The cowboy was clever. He hadn't been in the house for five minutes before he figured out that practical, down-to-earth Aunt Faye was the one he needed to win over.

"It's your decision, of course, Charlotte," Aunt Faye said slowly, "but don't you think you're being a little hasty, turning down an inheritance you know nothing about?"

"No."

"That's the thing about Gannens, Miss Darnelle. They can make up their mind in a flash. That way they don't have to be bothered about insignificant details like facts. Look at old Charlie. Without ever bothering to see his granddaughter, he made up his mind his son Chick couldn't possibly have fathered her. Yet a half-blind idiot can see Charlotte could have sat for the portrait of Charlie's first wife, Emily."

"I am not a Gannen," Charlotte said.

"Too bad Charlie's second wife didn't know that." Matthew Thorneton set his cup and saucer on a nearby table, carefully, as if he didn't trust himself with the delicate porcelain. "She wouldn't have wasted the past five years trying to convince Charlie to stop acting like an old fool and to acknowledge his granddaughter."

"I never asked for her help," Charlotte said, ignoring their silent, wide-eyed audience.

"That's right, you didn't." He stood up. "And I'm sure you don't give a damn that Charlie's will kicks her out on her ear."

Charlotte paled at the accusation. "I'm sorry, but—"

"You and Charlie. Two of a kind." He loomed over her. "So busy feeling sorry for yourselves about some imagined slight or other, you can't be bothered to consider anyone else's feelings."

Shaking with anger, Charlotte put down her cup. "Stop saying I'm in any way like Charles Gannen. I'm not."

"Charlie didn't take kindly to having his behavior questioned, either. He decided if his wife was so set on him doing the right thing by you, then he would." Matthew Thorneton's mouth hardened. "That's why he left everything to you. It was Charlie's way of telling his wife to mind her own business."

CHAPTER TWO

THERE was a long moment of horrified silence, and then Charlotte jumped to her feet. "Oh, no, you don't." She looked around the room. "He's trying to manipulate you into insisting I go. Ask yourselves why our hero here is riding to the rescue of this poor, noble woman. I'll tell you why. He said she's special to him." She gave Matthew Thorneton a frosty smile. "One has to wonder just exactly what that means."

His smile rivaled hers. "Come to Durango and find out."

"No."

Her grandma Darnelle frowned over the rim of her cup. "Charlotte, you always talk too fast for me. How could Mr. Gannen disinherit his wife? I thought she died years ago."

"He disinherited his second wife," Matthew said.

Aunt Faye looked at Matthew. "What happens if Charlotte doesn't go?"

"If she doesn't visit the ranch within the specified time limit, the estate goes to Connie Maywell, Chick Gannen's former fiancée. I'll be honest with you, Miss Darnelle, Charlie's will is irregular enough. If Charlotte hired a smart lawyer, she could probably tie up the estate for years. It would cost her a bundle of money, and in the end, she'd get no more than she can get now, which is everything. The simplest solution is for her to abide by her grandfather Gannen's last wishes, go to the ranch for two weeks and then sell to me. That way Charlie's widow wouldn't be dispossessed for even a minute."

"She's still living in the house?" Charlotte asked.

"She's staying on in a caretaker capacity until after your visit and the estate is settled. Would you like us to pay rent?" he asked coldly.

"Us? What did you do? Move in the day he died?"

"I've lived in the house for six years." He looked steadily at her. "Does one have to wonder what that means, too? Would you like to know where I sleep?"

"I couldn't care less." She could figure that one out herself. "But it certainly goes a long way toward explaining why he left her nothing."

"Charlotte!" her grandmother said in a shocked voice.

There was nothing pleasant about Matthew Thorneton's laugh as he picked up his hat. "I can't get over how much she thinks like Charlie did," he said to the room at large. "Thanks for dinner, ladies. If you have any questions, I'm staying at the Brown Palace hotel. Charlotte, I'll see you tomorrow."

"You will not."

"Tomorrow, and the next day, and the day after that. Lady, until you agree to come to Charlie's ranch, I'm going to be harder to get rid of than flies in a barnyard."

"Then you'd better buy the Brown Palace, because it'll be cheaper than renting a room every night the rest of your life. Charles Gannen never acknowledged me when he was living, and I refuse to acknowledge him just because he's dead."

"And to hell with everyone else involved."

"That's exactly right. To hell with your girlfriend."

"Chickie . . ."

"I'm sorry, Mother, but he has no right to judge me."

"I'm sure he wasn't judging you," Jewel said.

"Actually, I was." Matthew Thorneton measured Charlotte with hard eyes. "Charlotte may look like a sweet, old-fashioned girl, but beneath that frilly exterior is a marble-hearted, selfish, redheaded shrew. On top of which, she's a coward."

"My courage has nothing to do with—"

"I think it does. You're afraid to come to Durango."

"Don't be ridiculous." He couldn't possibly be that perceptive. "What would I be afraid of?"

"A soft, spoiled woman like you gets hysterical at the thought of getting a little dirt under your fingernails or smudging your pretty lace dresses. You don't have to worry, Ms. Darnelle. Charlie's place may not be up to your elegant standards, but we don't eat with our fingers or sleep in the barn. We even have indoor plumbing."

He was so far wrong, she felt almost giddy with relief. "Now you've spoiled my picture of your sunbonneted girlfriend, wearing patched dimity and scratching at the ground with a hoe."

"I don't know what the hell dimity is, but I do know—"

"Mr. Thorneton, Matthew, please. I know Charlotte is being somewhat contrary, but you must realize this comes as quite a shock to her."

"Don't apologize to him, Mother."

"Somewhat contrary is a filly who's acting skittish," Matthew Thorneton said. "Charlie's bulls are less stubborn than Charlotte."

"See?" Charlotte appealed to her mother. "He won't even admit you were subtly asking him to behave himself."

"Charlotte Mary Darnelle, your lack of a father is no excuse to behave as if I didn't bring you up right." Jewel's face was pink with embarrassment. "Matthew is a guest in our home."

For the second time in one evening Charlotte's behavior had rebounded on her mother. And it was all the cowboy's fault. Provoking her into thoughtless speech.

Not that her mother was likely to excuse her on that account. Knowing it was useless, Charlotte muttered, "It's all his fault. I want him to go away."

"I know you do, Chickie. You want the whole situation to go away." Jewel patted the sofa beside her. "Come here." When Charlotte complied, her mother reached over to caress her daughter's cheek with a shaking hand. "If you only knew how often I prayed for this. Your father loved the ranch. No, Chickie—" she correctly interpreted Charlotte's dismay "—I don't care what you do with the ranch, sell it, give it away, it doesn't matter. What does matter is learning about your father. Go for a visit. See the land Chick loved so much, where he grew up, his room. Some of his things may still be around. There must be pictures." After a moment she added softly, "You never knew your father, and I've been able to give you so little of him, a few memories, a couple of pictures—" She broke off.

Charlotte's heart sank. She wasn't the one who needed to know more about the man her mother had loved. She looked at her mother, at the brave smile quivering Jewel's lips, at the blue eyes glittering with unshed tears, and knew she'd lost.

They all knew it. Aunt Faye was the first to put it in words. "There's no point you hanging around waiting for her, Matthew. She'll need a few days, a week, to get ready. She can fly down. They do have an airport in Durango, don't they?"

"Yes. The stage stopped running years ago," he added dryly.

"Ellen's daughter is having a hard time right now with her husband out of work," Grandma Darnelle said. "She'll be happy to fill in at the store and earn a little extra cash."

"Call me before you leave Denver, Matthew," said Aunt Faye. "I'll give you her travel arrangements."

"A week, Faye?" Charlotte's grandmother was saying. "I don't know if that's enough time to get her things ready."

"She'll need new clothes." Charlotte's mother was radiant. "We can't have her showing up looking like a poor relation."

"Charlie's place is a working ranch," Matthew said. "All she needs are a few pairs of jeans."

"Men." Jewel gave him an indulgent smile.

"And a party dress," Charlotte's grandmother said. "You never know. A lady likes to be prepared."

"A party dress," Matthew repeated, shaking his head. His grin as he looked at Charlotte was half malice, half anticipation. "I can hardly wait to see you peeling potatoes or cleaning the barn wearing an outfit like the one you have on."

Charlotte couldn't abide people who gloated in victory. "Don't push your luck, cowboy. I'm coming to the ranch as the new owner, not as a hired hand. I'll come and I'll decide the ultimate disposal of the ranch. In the meantime, since your apparent position on the ranch is errand boy, perhaps it would be wise of you to dwell on the fact that owners run things, not the hired help." She gave him a blinding smile. "Your special friend, Mrs. Charles Gannen, is not the owner yet."

To his credit, Matthew Thorneton did not explode in the middle of the living room. Minutes later the solid front door closed carefully behind him. He'd thanked his hostesses politely. He'd even managed a civil farewell to Charlotte, if one ignored a parting look that positively scorched.

Charlotte relished the small triumph before heading for her bedroom to indulge in dark thoughts.

"I don't think deliberately alienating him is wise."
Aunt Faye stood in Charlotte's bedroom doorway.

"Why not?" Charlotte swung about. "What about
those cracks of his about my appearance?"

Her great-aunt surveyed her from head to toe. "You
don't exactly look like someone who's going to fit in on
a ranch. He's probably frightened to death wondering
what in the world he's going to do with you when you
get to Durango."

"I doubt if fear is in that man's vocabulary."

"All the same, I'm glad we sent you away to camp
all those summers. At least you won't embarrass yourself
on a horse. That should reassure him."

Charlotte smiled grimly at the framed ribbons she'd
won for horsemanship. "Since the last thing I'm
interested in doing is reassuring Matthew Thorneton..."
The plan came from nowhere, brilliant in its total clarity.
"I wonder. He did seem to dwell inordinately on my
clothing. I had the distinct impression that, given a choice
between eating live grasshoppers and having me
underfoot, Mr. Thorneton would pick the grasshoppers."

"Charlotte Mary Darnelle, I don't trust that look on
your face," Aunt Faye said sternly. "What are you
planning?"

Charlotte widened her eyes. "My vacation wardrobe,
of course. What else?"

Charlotte's stomach plummeted to the level of her
painted toenails as the plane dropped down on the large
mesa that was home to La Plata County Airport. Informed of the travel arrangements, Matthew Thorneton
had said they'd be expecting Charlotte. She intended to
meet every single one of his expectations. Circumstances
compelled Matthew Thorneton to allow her to invade
his sacred stomping ground, but no one could doubt he

viewed her visit with the same enthusiasm Charlotte reserved for dental appointments. The command visit didn't exactly thrill her, either. Forced into it, she'd be less than human if she didn't look around for someone to vent her frustration on.

Matthew Thorneton won the grand prize. Not only had he delivered the ultimatum and relished her unwilling surrender, from the moment of their meeting the arrogant cowboy had made it clear he considered her spoiled, selfish and a worthless piece of overdecorated fluff. Charlotte carefully retied the dainty bow at her lace-edged neckline as the plane taxied to a halt. On a scale of people whose opinions she cared about, cowboys rated absolute last. Which is why, instead of proving to him he was wrong about her, playing the role of pampered lady promised much more satisfaction. Charlotte had no intention of suffering alone. Making Matthew Thorneton absolutely miserable for the next two weeks might make being on the ranch almost bearable.

Aunt Faye insisted Charlotte was making Matthew Thorneton a scapegoat for the sins of the Gannens, but Aunt Faye hadn't been the recipient of Matthew Thorneton's contemptuous accusation that she'd shirked her family responsibilities. He'd even admitted he was sitting in judgment on her. He wasn't such a paragon himself. He was a cowboy, and cowboys always wanted something for nothing, a lesson she'd learned well from Charles and Chick Gannen. Charlotte intended this particular cowboy to pay for what he wanted, her ranch. She grinned. Being a thorn in Matthew Thorneton's side was worth infinitely more than mere dollars and cents. In the terminal, she spied him waiting on the other side of the gray double doors. His face was a study in disbelief and irritation as she made her way toward him.

He grabbed the larger of the two bags she was carrying. "At least you traveled light," he said by way of greeting.

"It's nice to see you again, too." Handicapped by her new four-inch-high-heeled sandals, she struggled to keep up with his long strides. "And thank you for asking, I did have a pleasant flight. And yes, I did travel light." Matthew headed for the glass doors that led outside. "All I checked was one suitcase and my trunk."

He stopped dead. "A suitcase and a trunk." Muttering under his breath, Matthew wheeled to his right and stalked down a hallway.

Assuming he was headed for the baggage claim area, Charlotte teetered along behind him, her ruffled peach skirt swirling around her calves.

"Want me to carry that?"

Charlotte looked down. The young boy at her side looked eagerly at her with warm brown eyes under wavy golden hair. He was all skinny arms and legs, his elbows and knees scratched. Charlotte caught her breath. Matthew Thorneton had said nothing of a son. Where did the child fit in? She nodded toward the man striding ahead of her. "You with him?" Her cool voice extinguished the friendly light in the boy's eyes. Charlotte hadn't come to win a popularity contest, but she felt as if she'd kicked a small puppy. She handed him her bag. "Thanks. My arm's about to fall off."

His face lit up again, and he hefted the bag. "Food?"

"Not hardly. Beauty creams, makeup, stuff like that."

His eyes widened. "All this?" At her nod, he said, "Aw, you're kiddin' me. Grandma doesn't have half this much stuff."

What about his mother? Instead of asking, Charlotte said, "Who are you? I'm Charlotte Darnelle."

"I know. I'm Timothy Thorneton. That is, Grandma calls me Timothy when she's mad at me."

Charlotte grinned in sympathy. "I know I'm in trouble when my mom calls me Charlotte Mary. What does your grandma call you when she's not mad?"

"Timmy." He wrinkled his nose in disgust. "My friends call me Tim. You can, too." He hesitated shyly. "If you want."

"I should think so. You're carrying my bag. That must make us friends."

"Dad said you was lucky you don't look like Grandpa Charlie. He told Grandma you're sorta pretty even if your hair's red." Innocently oblivious to the uncomplimentary nature of the remark he'd repeated, he added, "Your hair's the same color as Penny's and you got almost as many freckles as me."

"Grandpa Charlie," Charlotte repeated slowly. "You mean Charles Gannen was your grandpa?"

"Yup." A grin split his face from ear to ear. "Didn't you know me and you got the same grandpa?"

"No, I didn't." Shock chilled her voice. "I was under the impression I was Mr. Gannen's only grandchild."

Tim gave her an anxious look. "I don't have to share him."

"I have a feeling Charlotte isn't used to sharing."

They'd reached the baggage area. The scornful look on Matthew Thorneton's face told Charlotte he'd heard the end of their conversation and reached his own conclusions. She lifted her chin. "I certainly don't wish to share Mr. Gannen. Tim may have him for a grandfather all by himself. I was simply surprised after what you said last week."

"In Tim's case, Grandpa was an honorary title," he said shortly. "Which bag is yours?" A look of pained disbelief crossed his face. "Never mind. I can figure it out."

"Gosh," Tim said weakly, staring at the luggage carousel. "I thought you was just coming to visit."

"A lady has to dress," Charlotte said. Hauled down from the attic, covered in wallpaper printed with huge red cabbage roses, the large wardrobe trunk was attracting a great deal of notice. Matthew Thorneton might look nonchalant as he heaved it to the floor, but his tanned skin failed to hide the dusky pink tinging his cheeks. Charlotte could hardly wait for him to notice the suitcase. Tim saw it first and started giggling. Almost immediately he jammed his fist in his mouth and gave Charlotte an apologetic look. She winked at him.

He took the wink as permission and howled with laughter. "Over there, Dad. That one."

"I see it," came the response from between gritted teeth.

The suitcase had survived the trip amazingly well. Only one of the enormous pink bows had come untied. Charlotte was immensely pleased with herself. "Be careful. Don't scratch the trunk."

"How the hell am I supposed to get this stuff to the truck?"

"I assumed whoever met me would be prepared." Ignoring the militant look in Matthew's eyes, Charlotte took a deep breath and trilled, "Last week I wasn't too happy about coming, but now I'm here, I know it's going to be an absolutely enchanting visit."

"Enchanting," Matthew repeated sourly.

Smiling vaguely in his direction, Charlotte walked with Tim toward the parking lot. As curious as she was about the boy, she refrained from asking questions. She would have plenty of time at the ranch to ferret out the relationships. Tim led her to the now-familiar filthy pickup.

"I hope you weren't expecting a fancy stretch limo."

The cool, I-don't-give-a-damn voice came from behind her. Charlotte turned. Matthew had commandeered a loading dolly from somewhere and was lifting her luggage into the bed of the truck. "Did Mrs. Gannen tell you to pick me up in this or was that your own clever idea? I suppose it's some kind of test, a sort of ritual by dirt, so to speak."

He walked away with the dolly, saying over his shoulder, "There was no time to wash it."

Charlotte resisted an urge to make a face at his retreating back. "You first, kiddo," she said to Tim, gathering her skirt and petticoats in front of her. "Get in and haul me up."

By the time Matthew returned, they were both belted in the front seat of the pickup, a giggling Tim in the middle, little besides his nose sticking out from an unruly heap of starched crinolines. "Look at me, Dad."

Matthew scowled at Charlotte. "I don't suppose it occurred to you Tim might like to be able to breathe. Take those damned things off, and I'll tie them in back."

"It's OK." Tim bounced his arms up and down on the buoyant petticoats. "I think it's funny." His mind flitted to another subject. "How come you never visited us before, Charlotte?" As his dad opened his mouth, Tim quickly said, "She told me to call her that."

Charlotte looked over the boy's head. "Perhaps you'd prefer Cousin Charlotte."

"My preferences have never been considered in this matter," he said in a clipped voice.

"Nor were mine," Charlotte coolly reminded him before ignoring him in favor of his son. Tim needed little persuasion to show off his knowledge in front of the city slicker. His freckled face knew nothing of guile as he chattered about school and his horse while pointing out browsing deer and prairie dogs scurrying among their mounds beside the road.

Half listening to the small boy's conversation, Charlotte turned her face toward the passing landscape as the pickup bore her inexorably down off the mesa. The land was green and lush from spring rains. In the distance, dark, billowy storm clouds hung in the late afternoon sky, and the sharp, pungent odor of skunk stung her nostrils. Red-winged blackbirds took flight from the bank of a rushing river. Charlotte envied their freedom.

Durango was a kaleidoscope of color and sights, a larger river, lilacs in their last bloom, bustling traffic, businesses lining the highway, huge orange poppies, houses clinging to rugged cliffs, and then they were climbing again, red hills walling in the highway. On a different occasion Charlotte might have found beauty in the towering pines and tall cottonwoods and crashing river, but now even nature seemed inhospitable. The pickup crested the hill, and spread before them, fingers of bright green ranch land freckled with cows and horses reached up into the dark forested hills.

"Is this where we're going?" Charlotte asked Tim.

"Nah. It's a long way. Betcha can't wait to get there."

Fortunately the small boy didn't require an answer, his attention caught by a magpie feeding on a road kill. Charlotte resolutely focused on the beauty of her surroundings. In the distance the snow-capped San Juan Mountains loomed stark and forbidding. Huge patches of wild iris decorated the pastureland, the delicate blue blossoms in danger of being crunched beneath clumsy bovine hooves.

"See that?" Tim pointed straight ahead to a low-lying indigo silhouette bracketed by mesas and backlit by the setting sun. "That's the Sleeping Ute."

"Legend says he'll awaken some day to lead the Ute Indians against their enemies," Matthew added in his deep voice. He gave her a sidelong look. "I say, let sleeping giants lay."

"Or sleeping granddaughters," Charlotte said tartly. "Or them."

If Tim understood the undercurrents of their conversation, he dismissed them, pointing out some calves in a nearby pasture. Matthew slowed the pickup to turn off the main road. Pink wild roses and lavender-blue lupine failed to charm Charlotte. Not with the ranch and the second Mrs. Gannen still to come.

Matthew pulled into a ranch yard and brought the pickup to a halt. Dust settled behind them. Tim scrambled under the wheel and jumped from the truck in his father's wake. "I'll tell her she's here," the boy shouted, running for the house.

Matthew opened the door on Charlotte's side. His hand closed over the ankle she was extending toward the ground. "Tim's not part of Charlie's estate. Leave him alone."

His icy voice held Charlotte more immobile than the steel hand imprisoning her ankle. "I beg your pardon."

"You heard me. Tim doesn't need some silly female messing up his mind. He's a friendly, curious kid and too young to understand the way women like you think. Stay away from him."

Charlotte looked down her nose at the hard, closed face, her mind churning furiously with anger. She pasted a demure smile on her face. "My, oh, my, a misogynist. I never would have guessed. What with the second Mrs. Gannen and all." She fluttered her eyelashes. "This visit could be downright entertaining."

"You know, Charlotte, you make me think of a cream puff. Have you ever seen one after it's been stomped on?" A smile slashed across Matthew's face. "Play all the games you want with me—" he slid his fingers up and down her calf "—but leave Tim alone." He traced the strap of her sandal. "Call this a friendly warning, cream puff. Try to be less silly than these shoes."

He was being deliberately provocative. Knowing it and ignoring it were two different things, especially when his touch set her leg on fire and caused her stomach to react in alarming ways. Charlotte swallowed hard and stuck out her other foot, searching blindly for the step. "How nice that you intend to be friendly, Matthew."

Clasping her around the waist, he pulled her from the pickup truck, holding her so her mouth was level with his, her feet dangling inches above the ground. "You leave my son alone and I'll be just as friendly as you want, cream puff."

For a moment she thought he intended to kiss her, but then he lowered her slowly to the ground, the tips of her breasts grazing his chest, his gaze locked on her face. His brown eyes looked as warm and sultry as his voice sounded. His ears were tucked close to his head, the tops hidden by waves of brown hair that tempted a woman to run her fingers through them. His bottom lip was surprisingly full for a man's, and Charlotte wondered how it would feel pressed against her own lips. Immediately she understood why the second Mrs. Gannen had invited Matthew into her house six years ago. Muscles flexed beneath her fingers, and Charlotte realized she had a death grip on his upper arms. She dropped her hands and stepped back, praying her boneless legs would support her. Matthew released her waist and crossed his arms over his chest. The hint of amused triumph in his eyes put the stiffening back in her bones. The nerve of him, trying to control her through seduction. Obviously a skill he excelled in.

Reaching up, Charlotte lightly traced one of the grooves beside Matthew's mouth. "Will Tim's mother be friendly, too?"

All expression vanished from his face. "Tim's mother is dead."

The air smelled of dust spiced with the acrid pungency of sage. A grasshopper buzzed loudly in the stricken silence. Taking a deep breath, Charlotte followed Matthew to the back of the truck. Dirt invaded her sandals, the fine grit settling between her toes, a pebble finding its way under the ball of her foot. "I'm sorry, I—"

"Why?" The tailgate of the pickup crashed down. "Hoping to sow a few seeds of marital discord to stave off boredom?"

Charlotte felt hot color stain her cheeks. The notion had occurred to her. He'd never believe she'd instantly discarded it. "I'm sorry Tim lost his mother," she said stiffly.

He grabbed her two smaller bags. "Which brings us full circle. Leave Tim alone."

Charlotte showed him her back. Halfway to the house, he passed her.

"I'm so glad you came." A middle-aged woman stood on the porch beside Tim. Her smile was warm. "I apologize for not coming to the airport, but Matt had to pick up supplies at the feed store, and we wouldn't all fit in the pickup."

"I consider myself lucky Matthew needed supplies. I'm sure no one would have bothered to make an extra trip just for me."

The woman's smile momentarily faltered. "Timmy and I could hardly wait until you got here. We've been so anxious to meet you. Matt said you were pretty."

"'Sorta pretty,' I believe he said." Another time Charlotte would have felt badly betraying Tim by repeating his innocent remark, but now she was too beset by conflicting emotions to curb her impetuous speech. "Matthew obviously dislikes red hair—which I don't have, my hair is strawberry-blond—as much as he dislikes ruffled petticoats and stylish shoes, but Matthew is such an arrogant, surly excuse for a human being, I doubt he likes much of anything." Seeing the shock on the woman's face, Charlotte was ashamed of her outburst and added lamely, "I'm Charlotte Darnelle." As if she could be anyone else.

"I'm Helen Gannen," the woman said weakly.

"I'm right, aren't I, Grandma?" Tim looked at the woman. "Charlotte does look like she belongs on TV and her hair's the same color as Penny."

"Grandma?" Charlotte repeated. Too late she registered golden-brown eyes and chestnut brown hair streaked with gray.

"I beg your pardon," Matthew said in a sarcastic voice as he appeared through the front door. "Charlotte, allow me to introduce Charlie's second wife, Helen. Oh, and Charlotte, Helen is my mother. I may have neglected to mention that before."

Several hours later Charlotte propelled the old porch swing into motion to the accompaniment of creaking chains. Stray breezes brought the soft lowing of cattle and their less pleasant aroma. The growing darkness and solitude gave her an opportunity to sort out the information she'd been bombarded with since her arrival at Durango. Matthew had disappeared after dinner, and Helen was upstairs reading to Tim. Charlotte smiled. The boy had used Charlotte's visit to try to wangle a later bedtime. That he'd completely failed to sway his father didn't surprise Charlotte. She slapped at an annoying insect. Tim and his father had lived here since Matthew's wife had died when Tim was two. Helen watched over her grandson. The explanation had been lightly given, and Charlotte suspected there was more to the story, but Matthew's marriage was none of her business. It was more intriguing that a woman as nice and sweet as Helen had married a hard, opinionated man like Charles Gannen after they'd lost their respective spouses. Helen must have been twenty years younger than the rancher. Her first husband obviously had left her poorly provided for. Helen was probably used to arrogant, obnoxious, hard-bitten men. Like her son.

"Aren't you worried the night air might injure your delicate constitution or muss up your hair, cream puff?" The quiet, taunting question came out of the dark.

Charlotte tried to cover up her convulsive start by pushing the swing faster. "I'd be gratified by your concern for my health if I didn't know it was motivated by a fear I might drop dead of consumption or something two days before my term of imprisonment is up."

"Yeah, I'd hate to have gone to all the trouble of dragging you down here for nothing." Matthew pushed her to one side and sat down on the swing. The chains creaked ominously. Catching her swift glance upward, he said dryly, "It'll hold. You're in no danger from the swing falling."

"I'm sure you'll keep me safe. If I were killed falling from a horse or gored to death by a cow, you'd lose."

"Not if your two weeks were up. Your mom would inherit and she'd sell to me."

"I can't believe even you would say anything that cold-blooded."

"Why not? You know I want the ranch."

The flat statement was utterly convincing. Charlotte overcame an impulse to shiver and scoffed, "I guess anything can be believed of a man who'd lie about his own mother."

"I didn't lie about her."

"You know very well I thought she was someone else."

"Someone else like my live-in lover? I can't help how your mind works. I may be a dumb cowboy, but I'm not so dumb I couldn't guess you wouldn't come within a hundred miles of Charlie's place if you knew I wanted to buy it for my mother."

A sneaking suspicion he could be right kept Charlotte from arguing that particular point. "Honesty is always the best policy," she said virtuously.

"You might want to take that edict a little more to heart yourself, cream puff."

Charlotte froze. "Meaning?"

"Meaning maybe you ought to examine why you were so dead set against coming down here. There's no question that Charlie Gannen was your grandfather, and that he owed you for how badly he treated your mother and you. If he had left you nothing, I could understand your anger. What I don't understand is why you're so darned mad at him for leaving you everything."

Charlotte gripped her fingers together in her lap. "You think he left me everything?" His failure to answer goaded her into further speech. "My mother wasn't the official next of kin, so nobody notified her when Chick Gannen was killed. When his letters from Vietnam quit coming, she knew something was terribly wrong. He'd told her about his family in Durango, and she tracked down the phone number through the phone company. Charles Gannen answered the phone and told her his son was dead."

"That's a hell of a thing to hear over the phone."

Charlotte pulled distractedly at her fingers. "By then Mother was sure she was pregnant so she told Charles Gannen. Not because she wanted anything, but because she knew Chick was an only child, and she thought the prospect of a grandchild might ease his parents' grief. Aunt Faye said my mother turned white as a ghost and fell to the floor, her hands pressed against her stomach. Grandpa Darnelle grabbed the phone, and Charles Gannen repeated what he'd said to my mother. He called her a liar and a whore and accused her of having read about Chick's death and trying to pull a scam on a grieving family. He cursed her baby, if there was a baby and she wasn't making that up, too, and said if he heard from her again, he'd set the authorities on her."

Matthew laid a hand over Charlotte's restless fingers. "Charlie had a hard time coping with Chick's death."

She resented his defense of the old man. "By the time I was born, Mother had convinced herself Charles Gannen said those things because of shock and grief. She made a copy of one of Chick's letters where he talked about how they'd get married when he returned from Vietnam, and she sent it and a birth announcement to the Gannens. A lawyer returned them, along with a letter threatening everything from suing to having my mother declared unfit and me taken away from her. Not that they wanted me. I'd be given to some agency to be adopted out." She gave a harsh laugh. "War stole the man my mother loved. His father tried to steal her honor and self-respect."

"You have to understand how badly Charlie was hurt by what he saw as Chick's betrayal. Connie Maywell, your father's fiancée, was the daughter of the Gannens' oldest friends."

"I understand he was a mean and vindictive old man."

After a long moment, Matthew said, "There was nothing Charlie wouldn't do for a friend. To spare Connie, he never told the Maywells about you or your mother. Connie married and moved to California. Her parents are dead, or Charlie would never have played his trick with the will. Even after he changed it back, the risk of them learning about you would have been too great."

"I hate that will," Charlotte said fiercely. "I want to see the lawyer as soon as possible. I want to find out what my chances are of breaking the will."

"They're not very good. I went over that very thoroughly with Charlie's attorney."

"There must be something I can do. I hate dancing to Charles Gannen's tune. I ought to stay one week and take all the photographs and gather all the information and soak up all the atmosphere my mother could ever want. And then leave."

"What would that prove?" Matthew laid his arm along the back of the swing.

"It would prove, dead or alive, he can't snap his fingers and have me come running."

"If you're talking revenge, the best revenge is you outlived him, and he had no other blood relative to leave his holdings to." Matthew wrapped his hand around the back of her neck. "Why don't you relax and enjoy your vacation, cream puff?"

"Don't call me that." Matthew's hand was warm. She felt the calluses on his palm. Each movement of the swing sent the smell of his soap eddying through the air.

"Why not?" He trailed his fingers behind her ear. "Cream puffs are sweet and luscious-looking. Fancy pastries for special occasions. As a boy I could never decide if I wanted to nibble on one, take big bites or try to swallow the cream puff whole." He tugged a curl from the top of her head and wound it around his finger. "What do you think, Charlotte?"

"I think cream puffs are fattening and high in cholesterol." The sound of creaking chain was as mesmerizing as the black velvet sky studded with diamond stars. "They clog your arteries."

Shifting position, Matthew brought up his other hand and rubbed his thumb slowly over her bottom lip. "Maybe clogged arteries aren't such a bad way to go." The swing slowed. "Are freckles fattening, too? Do you know you have one right here?" Matthew pressed his thumb below the corner of her mouth.

Charlotte struggled against words that flowed over her like silk. "It's too dark out here to see freckles." She knew because his face was in shadow, denying her any clue to his thoughts.

"I'd be surprised if you didn't have a freckle there." Matthew laughed softly. "Tim's freckles taste like dirt and grape juice." The swing stopped. "I'll bet yours don't."

She felt his warm breath against her face, and then his lips were pulling at the edges of her mouth. "I don't have freckles there," she managed to say.

CHAPTER THREE

"I SAW one earlier," Matthew muttered against her skin. "And one here and here—" he trailed his lips across her cheekbone "—and one here under your ear. Not one of them tastes like grape juice." He ran his tongue down the side of her neck.

"I use peach facial cleanser," she said prosaically. She hadn't come to the ranch to play, and Matthew was hardly her type. He was, however, up to something. She decided to find out what.

He laughed softly. "I hope peach cleanser doesn't remove freckles." He slid his mouth over her shoulder. "The day we met I could see freckles through the thin material of your dress. I couldn't help but wonder how far down they went."

Heat from his mouth warmed her skin through her blouse. Tiny shivers danced down Charlotte's spine as his fingers lightly probed her hair, sending curls tumbling to her shoulders. Her type or not, Matthew had an unsettling effect on her, his touch puddling her insides. He shifted and the swing moved, sliding her closer to him. His hip scalded her through her dress. It was time to stop. "I think—"

"Don't think. Just—" his hands cradling her face, he tipped her head back "—this."

Expecting a hard, demanding kiss, Charlotte was disarmed by the light feathering of his lips against hers. She melted into his embrace to be jolted by major volts of electricity as Matthew slid his tongue along her bottom lip. Jerking away, she scooted to the other end of the

44

swing. Matthew said nothing. With shaking hands, Charlotte gathered up the hairpins he'd dropped in her lap. "In Denver you made it clear you found me as appealing as moldy bread. I can't believe a week later you're suddenly attracted to me. I suppose the kiss was because you felt sorry for poor, fatherless me after hearing my sad story."

"You don't need me feeling sorry for you, cream puff. You do a good job of that all by your lonesome. The kiss was no act of charity. It was just a kiss."

"If I hadn't stopped you, I hate to think how far you were willing to go."

Matthew stretched out long legs. "That's the difference between you and me. I kind of like thinking about it."

"Did you also think I might be susceptible to the same excessive passions my mother was susceptible to? That because I'm illegitimate, I have no moral backbone?"

"Damn it, Charlotte, I didn't think anything of the sort. It's not freckles you have on your shoulder—it's the world's largest chip."

The genuine astonishment in his voice acquitted him of that particular sin, but from the time she'd arrived, Matthew had snarled and barked like a rabid dog. Except when warning her away from his son. Then he'd used his masculinity in an attempt to manipulate her. What did he want from her now? Suddenly she heard her own voice saying she ought to leave before the two weeks were up. Matthew Thorneton thought he could seduce her into staying until he got what he wanted. And what he wanted wasn't Charlotte Darnelle. He wanted the ranch. Of course he'd deny it if Charlotte had any intention of accusing him. Sometimes there were more effective ways of making people pay. "Never mind, Matthew." She gave a little sniff. "It's all right. With my parentage, I'm used

to boys testing me. I admit I thought you were above..."
She let her voice trail off pathetically.

"You read too much into what happened."

"I guess I misunderstood what you meant when you
said you wondered how far down my freckles went. Boys
have been saying that to me since I was sixteen, but that's
no excuse for my jumping to conclusions." She hung her
head. "I should have known you were too mature to try
to seduce me on a porch swing."

"I thought we were mutually enjoying ourselves. I
don't remember you slapping my face."

"Are you saying I led you on? That I'm a—a..." The
tiny sob was an artistic masterpiece.

"Oh, hell," he said roughly. "Don't make so damned
much of a simple kiss. If it bothered you so much, maybe
we'd better stay out of each other's way the rest of your
visit."

Charlotte swallowed a giggle. So that was Matthew's
ploy. Unable to believe anyone would whistle away an
inheritance, his worry wasn't that she'd leave, but that
she'd be a pest. Under normal circumstances, Matthew
Thorneton not crossing her path for the entire two weeks
of her enforced stay would have suited her just fine.
Except, knowing it would suit him even better, she had
no intention of hiding in her room. "No, Matthew, you
were right. I made too much fuss over a little kiss. The
next time a man kisses me, I won't behave like a silly
schoolgirl." Squaring her shoulders, she added, "Now
that we understand each other, Matthew, and I know
I'm in no danger of being seduced by you, I'll count on
you showing me around tomorrow."

"I'd rather walk barefoot into a den of rattlers." His
thin veneer of amiability had definitely cracked.

Charlotte grinned in the dark. It was time to remind
Matthew Thorneton who had the upper hand. "If that's

the way you feel about it. Of course, if I'm not happy here, I probably won't stay. And if that Maywell woman gets the ranch, well, you could hardly expect me to write a letter of recommendation for an uncooperative employee, could you?'' She slipped out of the swing. ''Good night, Matthew.''

''If Charlotte doesn't get her way, Charlotte goes home? All right. You win.'' He paused. ''I hope you won't regret it.''

''I appreciate your cooperation, Matthew. I may have to ask the lawyer about a bonus for you.''

The swing creaked loudly. ''Don't worry about a bonus for me, cream puff. I'll make sure I get everything owed me.''

Charlotte ignored the soft menace in his voice. Matthew Thorneton might not like her, but he needed her, and he'd take very good care to insure she stayed for two weeks. ''I'll see you in the morning. We can make plans then.''

''In the country we get up early.''

''You forget I'm a working woman,'' she gently chided him, moving toward the screen door. ''I'm used to rising early.''

''You were right about one thing and wrong about another.''

Charlotte paused, her hand on the door handle. ''Was I?''

''Back in Denver you said you weren't a good enough actress to play the big deathbed scene. You're right. You'd overplay the scene. As you did just now.''

She didn't bother to deny it. ''And what was I wrong about?''

''I didn't say you were sort of pretty. I said you were pretty if a man likes red hair and freckles.''

Her fingers tightened on the handle. "Good night, Matthew."

"Aren't you going to ask if I do?"

Not in a million years, Charlotte thought as she slowly descended the staircase the next morning. She hadn't answered Matthew or asked the question he'd wanted her to ask because she already knew the answer. Not that she was the least bit interested in his opinion of red hair. Especially since hers was strawberry-blond. Let Matthew Thorneton think he'd had the last word. He'd find out soon enough Charlotte wasn't some naive country girl he could manipulate with a few kisses and threats. She was his employer, and he'd better behave accordingly. She looked forward to a day of reminding him. For a hired hand, he was entirely too outspoken and determined to have things his way. She entered the dining room, yawning widely.

"Gosh, Charlotte, what took you so long? I was 'fraid I'd have to go before you got up," Tim cried.

"Charlotte's definition of early rising differs somewhat from ours," Matthew said in a sardonic voice.

Helen tapped Tim's shoulder. "Ten minutes until the school bus."

"I want to show Snowball to Charlotte."

"Snowball?" Charlotte sent a vague smile in the direction of a scowling Matthew.

Tim stuck his arm in her face. "My rat," he said proudly.

Charlotte took one look at the tiny head peering out from Tim's sleeve and put down her coffee. She sensed Matthew watching her reactions with keen anticipation. "He's charming," she said faintly, edging her chair back.

"You can play with him while I'm at school."

"You're very kind. Does he bite?"

"No," Tim said in disgust. "He's not that kind a rat."

"How nice," Charlotte said. "Hadn't you better hurry so you don't miss your bus?"

"Wanna hold him?"

"No. Thank you. Not before breakfast."

"OK. See ya." Tim tore from the room, his grandmother following more slowly.

Matthew chuckled.

Charlotte looked at him. "What's so amusing?"

"Your face when Tim shoved the rat in it. How do you like country life so far, Charlotte?"

"I like it just fine. As for the rat, I'm sure he's a delightful pet."

"Wait until you see his tail. It's long and scaly. Makes me think of a snake winding around your arm." Matthew sipped his coffee, eyeing her over the rim of the mug. "Mom gets annoyed with Tim, the way he lets Snowball run wild through the house."

"Run wild?"

The corners of Matthew's mouth twitched. "He's quite a climber. Once when Tim had him out, he disappeared and we turned the house upside down looking for him. Searched everywhere. We'd about given up when he leaped down on Mom's head. You'll never guess where he was." He looked expectantly at her.

She obliged him by asking, "Where?"

"On top of the tall bookcase in Chick's room, the room you're sleeping in now."

"The room I'm in," Charlotte repeated hollowly.

"It was the darnedest thing. We never did figure how that rat got in there with the door closed. There must be some hole we don't know about. He'd sure been busy. We could see where he'd climbed up on the bed and tunneled under the covers." Matthew set his coffee down and stood up. "He's a clever fellow."

But not half as clever as you think you are, Charlotte thought as Matthew left. He was obviously annoyed about having his day conscripted by his new employer. Thus the petty attempt to frighten her with the rat. She sipped her coffee. Matthew'd better be careful his childish revenge didn't backfire and scare her away before he was willing for her to go. One had to wonder when that would occur to him. She reached for a muffin.

"If you insist on seeing the place, I thought the best way to do so would be from the back of a horse." Matthew stood in the doorway. "Of course, if you've changed your mind and would prefer to spend the day laying around the house, I'd understand. Riding can be a dirty and dusty business."

"How sweet of you to worry about me, but I'd love to ride. Of course, I'll have to change."

Matthew visibly ground his teeth. "Do you think you might be ready by lunchtime?"

"You're such a tease, Matthew. It will only take me an hour or so to change."

"An hour or so."

She beamed at him. "I'll hurry." He turned on his heel and stomped down the hall. Charlotte buttered her muffin. She'd need to be well-fortified to face the day. She had a feeling Matthew hadn't forsaken his plan to convince her to stay in the house—and out of his way.

Two hours later she picked her way carefully across a wide expanse of dirt and gravel. Matthew was waiting for her at the corral behind the barn. Charlotte regretted leaving her camera in her room. The stunned look on Matthew's face when he saw her was priceless. "Here I am—" she gave him a wide smile "—and only a few minutes late."

"What on earth are you dressed for? A Halloween party?"

"I know, the hat doesn't quite go with the trousers." Reaching up, she jammed a pin more securely among the huge lavender fabric flowers that decorated the wide-brimmed straw hat. "With my delicate complexion, I have to be so careful."

"I told you to bring jeans."

"These looked so much smarter." Charlotte brushed an imaginary piece of dirt from her dark green jodhpurs. "The minute I saw some on a woman in a magazine— she was standing beside a horse—I knew they were exactly the thing to wear riding. Is that horse for me? It's beautiful. Is it a girl?"

Matthew patted the large, muscular gray. "Jay's a gelding, and I'm riding him."

"Gelding?" She could hardly wait to hear Matthew's answer.

"Let's just say ol' Jay here will never be a daddy."

Charlotte schooled her face to remain blank. "Why? Doesn't he like lady horses?"

Matthew frowned. "Didn't you ever have a cat or dog while you were growing up?"

"No, but what that has to do with... Oh, I see." She arched a supercilious eyebrow. "If I had, we certainly wouldn't have discussed that sort of thing in polite company." She could almost see the steam coming from Matthew's ears. Before he could erupt, she changed the subject. "What am I going to ride?"

His eyes narrowed. "Have you ever ridden before?"

She smiled confidently. "I've watched lots of television."

Muttering under his breath, Matthew wrapped the horse's reins over the top rail of the corral and disappeared into the barn, his back and shoulders rigid.

The upcoming ride showed promise. Tamping down her anticipation, Charlotte stroked the gray's velvety nose. Nearby a cloud of small cream-colored butterflies took flight. About twenty feet away a meadowlark sat on a fence post, puffed out his bright yellow chest and threw his distinctive song into the air, the trilling notes unimpeded by the huge worm hanging from his beak. Swallows swooped overhead and a pair of robins flew past. Shaded by tall pines, the ranch house crowned a knoll. The barn sat midway between the house and a cottonwood-lined stream, with various outbuildings scattered around. One picturesque, tumbledown shack had been taken over by a climbing rosebush loaded with yellow blooms. Charlotte lifted her face, soaking up the warm sunshine. Hearing Matthew's voice, she quickly stepped away from the gelding.

A light chestnut mare followed Matthew from the barn, placing her hooves daintily on the ground. Arching her neck, she neighed softly at the gray. Charlotte didn't have to fake her response. "He's beautiful."

"She. Her name is Penny." Matthew's eyes didn't quite meet Charlotte's.

"Penny." Charlotte giggled. "I see what Tim meant. We do have almost the same color of hair." She slanted Matthew a quick look. "Did you hope that would annoy me?" She stepped quickly back as he led the mare toward her.

"She won't bite." He ignored the question.

"She looks much bigger close up," Charlotte said doubtfully.

"She's the sweetest-tempered horse around. Riding her is like sitting in a rocking chair." Matthew slipped the reins over Penny's head and handed them to Charlotte. Walking over to his own mount, he untied him and swung lightly up. Leather creaked as he settled into the saddle. "Well?" He guided the large gelding over to where Charlotte stood.

Charlotte retreated before the large horse. "Well, what?"

"I thought you'd watched a lot of television. Let's go." When she didn't move, he said, "Put your foot in the stirrup, that thing there, hang on to the saddle so you don't fall over. OK, grab hold of the saddle horn, that—" he pointed again "—and pull yourself up, throwing your right leg over."

A large fly buzzed past Charlotte's nose. Penny twitched and swished her tail. Charlotte jumped out of the way. "I don't think she wants me to ride her."

"She's shooing away flies. Do as I said and you'll be fine. She won't move away."

Charlotte grabbed the saddle horn and tightened the reins in her hand. Penny sidestepped. "She won't hold still."

"That's because you pulled on the reins." Matthew swung down from his horse and dropped the reins to the ground. "Put this hand here and grab the back of the saddle with your other hand. Give me your foot. Not your right one. Your left one. OK. Up you go. Uh, Charlotte, you're supposed to put your other leg over the horse, not your head and body."

"Don't just stand there laughing, do something." Penny stood patiently, looking back at her strange rider. Charlotte was positive the mare was rolling her eyes in disbelief.

Taking firm hold of Charlotte's belt, Matthew pulled her upright. She flailed the air with her arms as he threw her right leg over the saddle. Capturing her windmilling arms, he anchored her hands firmly on the saddle horn. "Stand up so I can see if your stirrups are the right length. OK, sit." He adjusted each side. "Relax."

"It's awfully far down." She waited until he'd remounted. "Matthew, I lost my hat when I was getting on."

Back on the ground Matthew scooped up her hat and handed it to her. Charlotte draped the reins over the mare's neck, and holding the hat with one hand, searched with the other for the pins to skewer the hat in place. Matthew vaulted into his saddle, and his horse moved forward. Penny followed. "Whoa, horse, whoa!" Charlotte shrieked, grabbing for the saddle horn with both hands. "Matthew!"

Halting the gray, he turned around, resting one hand on the back of his saddle. "What's the matter?"

"I'm not ready to go yet. Tell her to hold still."

He reached for the reins. "Fix the damned hat." When she'd finished, he slapped the leather reins against her palms. "Use these to guide her and pull back when you want to stop. Gently. Penny has a soft mouth. You're not stopping a runaway train. OK. Give her a little nudge with your knee. Easy. We'll just walk 'em, now." He set off.

"Matthew. I hate to bother you..."

"Now what?"

"I dropped one of the leash things."

"They're called reins, Charlotte."

An hour later as she followed Matthew down a faint trail, Charlotte conceded she'd underestimated him. That he hadn't shoved her off a cliff long ago testified to a stubborn nature that refused to accept defeat. Or to enormous patience. Tim came to mind. "I'll bet you're a good father," she said without thinking.

Matthew turned his horse in a circle and reined in beside her. "What did you say?" he asked warily.

Darn. She hadn't meant to express the thought out loud. Matthew was waiting for an explanation. "You heard me," she said tartly. "Tim is obviously a healthy, happy boy who's friendly and outgoing, so that makes you a good father. Under the circumstances, it can't be easy for you."

"Circumstances?" His voice was tight.

"Being a single parent. I know your mother must be a tremendous help, but you have to make all the difficult decisions." Annoyed she started this conversation, she added awkwardly, "Being the child of a single parent, I have some idea of the difficulties..." She shrugged and urged Penny on.

Matthew guided his horse beside her. "I suppose you had it pretty rough as a kid."

"Certainly not. Illegitimate children love feeling different." In the blink of an eye Matthew presented her with his back and Jay's rump. Which she deserved, Charlotte admitted. Her past wasn't his fault. "Matthew," she said tentatively.

He didn't stop his plodding horse. "Those flowers are lupine, and I've already picked you some."

She urged Penny up beside the gray. "I guess you could say I'm a tad sensitive about my parentage." It was as close as she could come to an apology.

Matthew rested his hands on his saddle horn. "I never heard how Chick and your mom met."

"A girlfriend of Mom's talked her into going to the Denver Stock Show. Mom was trying on cowboy hats and Chick Gannen walked by and asked why a pretty girl like her didn't have a beau. He talked her into letting him buy her a cola, and one thing led to another." Charlotte drew circles on Penny's neck with the ends of the reins. "He was on leave before going to Vietnam, and he was at the rodeo hazing as a favor for a steer-wrestling friend whose regular hazer had a family emergency. You probably know a steer wrestler needs a hazer to keep the steer going straight, but all my mother knew about cows was hamburger comes from them. Mom had never been on a horse and didn't like Western movies, but she went to the stock show every night that week." Charlotte watched some crows flying raucously overhead. "Mom was hardly the person one would expect a cowboy to fall for. I'm sure his fiancée was more suitable."

Matthew shrugged. "Chick and Connie Maywell grew up together. Mom says they got engaged because their folks pushed them into it. She said Chick and Connie liked each other but they weren't in love."

"Love." Charlotte smiled tightly. "I think Mom fell in love with the romantic image of a cowboy. Mom insisted Chick Gannen looked better on a horse than John Wayne." She ran her fingers through the mare's mane. "Mom has a photograph of him on that horse. It wasn't his horse, but his friend's." Penny twitched, shaking off a fly. "When I was little, I was always asking Mom the horse's name, but she couldn't remember." Almost to herself, Charlotte added, "It's silly, but I used to hate not know—" She caught herself. Matthew Thorneton would think she was a complete moron if she confessed how much it had bothered her not knowing the horse's name. Penny swished her tail, and an unseen hummingbird whistled shrilly past. The air smelled of pine and sage and sweet clover.

Leather creaked as Matthew shifted in his saddle. "Chick used to haze occasionally for Bud Adamly. Maybe Bud will remember the stock show and the name of the horse."

"Don't be silly. It's childish. You don't need to bother."

"It's no bother."

"He probably doesn't even remember."

"Probably not."

Charlotte looked around for a new topic. "What pretty blue flowers."

"They're flax. You have some there." He nodded toward the bunch of wildflowers tied to her saddle. His eyes narrowed as he caught sight of her right hand resting easily on her thigh. His gaze moved to her left hand holding the reins as she guided the mare with a slight flick of her wrist. "You're doing pretty good for a greenhorn."

Inwardly cursing herself for being so preoccupied with their conversation that she'd totally forgotten her role, Charlotte visibly preened. "I guess I'm a born rider. If only Penny didn't keep growing wider." She stood gingerly in the stirrups to stretch, at the same time unobtrusively nudging Penny with her heel. Penny obediently moved forward. Charlotte squealed and clutched at the saddle horn, pulling on the reins at the same time. Penny stopped abruptly, and Charlotte pitched forward over the horse's neck.

"You're a born rider, all right," Matthew said solemnly. "You OK?"

"Certainly, I'm OK." Charlotte sat up and pushed her hat off her forehead, settling it firmly atop her head. "I was merely checking to see if I could ride and floss my teeth with Penny's mane at the same time. If you're interested, the answer is no."

"I'll keep that in mind. Ready?" At her nod, he rode off slowly.

Penny looked around and tossed her head. "Don't tell me you're shaking off a fly," Charlotte said to the horse. "That's a look of disgust if I ever saw one."

Matthew was already at the corral loosening the cinch on his saddle when Charlotte rode up. "To get down, just reverse the process." He didn't look up.

"I wish you'd mentioned that sooner," Charlotte said in a plaintive voice.

Matthew turned around, saw her and immediately swung back to face his horse. His shoulders were still shaking as he ducked under Penny's neck. "I'm afraid to ask."

"It wasn't easy," she tartly defended herself. "I swung my leg around and both legs were on the same side of Penny, but I had my back to her looking down at the ground and that didn't seem right so I swung one leg over and..." She clutched the back of the saddle, looking at the mare's tail in vague surprise.

"I can't remember the last time I had such an—" Matthew rested a hand on Penny's withers and looked at Charlotte "—interesting ride."

"Very amusing. Help me down."

"Swing your leg around, and grab on to my shoulders." When she'd followed his instructions, he reached up and clasped her around the waist. "I hope you won't be too sore to ride again with me tomorrow."

A more insincere sentiment Charlotte had never heard uttered. She batted her eyelashes at him. "After lunch I'll have a good long rest and I'll be fine."

Matthew's hands tightened. "Good. Since you did so well today, we might take a longer ride tomorrow. Maybe move a little faster. If you're still tender, a good trot will jar the soreness right out of those muscles."

"Do you really think so, Matthew?" Charlotte asked artlessly. His strategy was flagrantly obvious. No wonder he'd been so patient this morning. Matthew Thorneton was counting on her lily-livered constitution, not to mention tender bottom, to make her shelter in the ranch house for the remainder of her two-week stay. The really insulting part was he wasn't even bothering to make things tough for her. Of course, he couldn't go too far and risk her running back home to Denver. Charlotte gave him a warm smile.

An answering smile curved Matthew's mouth. "We don't get women like you—" he lifted her from Penny's back "—around here much."

Charlotte bent her head to look into his face. "What kind of woman am I?"

"Soft, sweet-smelling." He ran a finger under her lacy blouse collar. "Pink cotton candy, the lady on a chocolate box, the kind a boy dreams about. Silky lace nighties and perfumed sheets. Not a woman for shoveling out stalls or facing over the breakfast table, but a woman for loving on warm summer nights."

Charlotte dropped her eyes to hide a flash of anger. "That's very pretty talk, Matthew." The open V of his faded blue shirt exposed skin tanned to a golden brown. "But you make me sound rather insubstantial."

"Dream ladies usually are." He tipped up her chin. "Although I don't remember any of the ladies of my boyhood dreams having freckles. Maybe I didn't look closely enough." Shoving back his hat, he lowered his head.

"I thought last night we settled you weren't going to kiss me anymore, Matthew."

"We settled that the next time a man kissed you, you weren't going to act like a silly schoolgirl."

He was as subtle as a sledgehammer. Charlotte decided she'd better find out what else was brewing under his cowboy hat. He tasted of mint. The smells of the stable yard faded as the subtle scent of soap mingled with the warm smell of his skin. The Colorado sunshine directly overhead bathed her with heat. Charlotte slid a hand up his neck and pressed it against his cheek. He'd missed a tiny patch of beard in shaving, and the bristles rasped the sensitive skin of her palm. His warm, solid body curved protectively around her, filling her with a sense of safety and belonging. The well-washed denim of his shirt felt soft and comforting beneath her fingers. She slipped the fingers of one hand between the buttons of his shirt and was rewarded by the silken warmth of his chest. Matthew's mouth moved over hers and then his tongue slid between her lips.

Sometime later Matthew lifted his head. "It's a damned shame I have to live with Mom for Tim's sake."

Charlotte toyed with one of his shirt buttons. "Why do you say that?"

"Because I'd enjoy sharing my bed with a certain pretty lady. I'd like to count her freckles." He trailed a finger across Charlotte's cheek. "All of them."

CHAPTER FOUR

CHARLOTTE went very still. Matthew's provocative declaration went beyond frightening her into staying out of his way. Stiffening her arms, she broke free of his loose embrace. "I don't believe I ever indicated bedding the boss is part of your job description."

"I'm not averse to putting in a little overtime."

She could almost believe he was serious. Which made no sense. Even if he could coax her into his bed, which he couldn't, what could he hope to gain? It would be prudent to squash this little idea before he went too far. "Your attempts to seduce me, Matthew, are a total waste of your time." She'd only kissed him to find out what he was up to. His kisses were pleasant—well, maybe more than pleasant, but that was irrelevant.

"Why don't you let me be the judge of that?" He aimed a sensual smile at her mouth. "I thought my time was rather well spent."

Charlotte felt the color highlighting her cheeks. "I allowed you to kiss me because it amused me. I admit—" she fiddled with Penny's bridle "—the experience was somewhat pleasant, but I'm not looking for a two-week fling, and I'm not so simpleminded that a couple of kisses and some heavy breathing will blind me to what you're really after."

"And what would that be?"

"You're determined I carry out the conditions of Charles Gannen's will for your own selfish purposes. Your problem is, I couldn't care less if you get the ranch."

61

His eyes narrowed. "I want this ranch, Charlotte, and I intend to get it. One way or the other."

"If you wanted it so badly, you should have convinced him to will it to you," she snapped. Enlightenment burst over her. "I see," she said slowly. "It must have been quite a disappointment to have hung around all this time thinking Charles Gannen would leave his ranch to your mother, and by extension to you. Undoubtedly you worked hard for him and deserved some consideration, but you should have realized Charles Gannen and fairness were total strangers. While I can certainly testify to that, I feel no obligation to right any wrongs he perpetuated."

"Are you telling me you won't sell me the ranch?"

"Sell? Or give? I doubt very much a hired hand makes enough money to buy a ranch of any size these days. Isn't that what all your heavy-handed seduction is about?" Charlotte absently combed Penny's mane. "We both know you're not the least bit attracted to me. You thought you could seduce me into handing over the ranch to your mother for little or no payment. I'm afraid, cowboy, you rate your charms a little high."

He pulled his hat low over his forehead. "At least I don't accuse a woman of ulterior motives every time she kisses me."

Undoubtedly because he assumed every woman who kissed him was madly in love with him. She flicked some horsehair from the sleeve of her blouse. "I'm sure you need your job, so I'll forget about this episode."

The ensuing silence was broken by Penny's soft nickering as the mare rubbed her nose on Matthew's shoulder. Matthew's eyes were shaded by his wide-brimmed hat. "I suggest, cream puff," he said levelly, "you get that fancy, pampered bottom of yours up to the house before I decide what I want from you isn't

worth putting up with you for one more second.''
Grabbing Penny's reins, he led both horses toward the
barn.

Charlotte refused to let him think he intimidated her.
"What about Penny?'' she called after him. ''Aren't I
supposed to give her a bath or something after a ride?''
Matthew ignored her.

Charlotte outlined her lips in pale coral and bared her
teeth at the mirror, checking for lipstick smears. She
hoped Matthew's teeth were in as good condition.
Leading the horses to the barn, he appeared to be
grinding all the enamel from his molars. He hadn't liked
discovering Charlotte had figured out his scheme. For
a minute she'd feared for the horses' well-being, but decided Penny wouldn't be drooling all over Matthew as
if he were the herd stallion if Matthew were the type to
mistreat valuable animals.

Matthew had not joined Charlotte and Helen at lunch.
Fortunately his mother hadn't questioned his absence,
so Charlotte had been spared the need to explain
Matthew was pouting. Charlotte ran her fingers over the
ornate pattern of her great-grandmother's silver-backed
hand mirror. If she was honest with herself, she'd admit
Matthew's kisses affected her more than she liked. Surely
an attraction to cowboys couldn't be inherited, like blood
type or eye color. Just because her mother had been putty
in the hands of a handsome cowboy—Charlotte was
proof of that—didn't mean Charlotte had to go weak in
the knees at the sight of low-slung blue jeans and outsize
hats.

Opening a flacon of perfume, Charlotte absently
dabbed some on her pulse points. One day down and
thirteen to go. In other circumstances she might have
enjoyed the visit. The sky was blue, the air was clear,

colts were frisky and calves were adorable. The danger was in succumbing to feeling pride of ownership. She was no more than a tourist, passing through. All the silver and crystal dressing table appointments, all the lace pillows and flowered silk scarves over lampshades, all the family photographs in antique frames couldn't hide the fact that beneath the accessories hauled here from Denver in her trunk was a room Charles Gannen had never wanted to see her in. The ranch was no more a part of her life history than a trip to the moon.

Charlotte soothed an errant eyebrow. The mere suggestion of possibly keeping the ranch herself would be enough to set Matthew foaming at the mouth. She toyed with the idea. Men such as Matthew and the Gannens, father and son, assumed they could rearrange life to suit themselves. The Gannen men were beyond her reach, but it wouldn't hurt for Matthew to learn a small lesson in humility.

Standing, she stepped into her dress with its dropped waist and pale green floral print cotton and wide, creamy Battenberg lace collar. Matthew would undoubtedly think the old-fashioned, feminine dress suited a cream puff. Charlotte smiled. Men like Matthew underestimated cream puffs. Tomorrow she'd make plans for seeing Charlie Gannen's lawyer and discover for herself the exact worth of the estate she was due to inherit. The ranch meant nothing to her, and in the end, she supposed she'd sell it to Matthew if he could meet her asking price.

Charlotte's smile switched to a thoroughly unladylike grin. Negotiating with Matthew Thorneton when she had the upper hand promised to be entertaining. True to his name, he had been a thorn in her side from the first letter he'd sent her about her grandfather's illness. Since then his transgressions had multiplied—the second, lecturing letter, his forcing her to come to the ranch and his behavior since she'd arrived. He was a true cowboy, thinking because he filled out a pair of jeans nicely, had a devastating way of kissing and looked terrific on a horse...

Charlotte shook her head and plopped herself on the dressing table stool. If she wanted those kinds of fantasies, she could rent a Western video. She pinned a cameo at the deep V of her collar. Matthew was hardly a heroic figure. For heaven's sake, the man had to be over thirty years old, and he still lived with his mother. She chose to ignore the reason for Matthew's style of living.

The reason knocked loudly at her door. "You in there?"

Charlotte swung around. "Come in."

Tim peeked his head in. At her smile, he advanced the rest of the way. Animal-like, he sniffed the air. "Gosh. It stinks in here."

Charlotte laughed. "You wait a few years and you'll be singing a different tune. I see you have your friend with you." The rat was sniffing the air in almost perfect imitation of the boy whose shoulder he rode on.

Tim's eyes widened as he looked around. "This room sure looks different. Kinda sissy." He jumped up on the bed. "Grandpa Charlie's son, Chick, was your dad, wasn't he?"

"So I'm told."

"You remember him?"

Charlotte ignored the dirty tennis shoes on the washable white coverlet. "I never knew him. He was killed in a war before I was born." Her mother had known him a week. Jewel's sole mementos of her only love were three pictures and a few letters. And Charlotte.

Tim lifted the rat from his shoulder to his lap, curling the animal's tail around his hand. "If you was two when he died, would you remember him?"

At the odd note in Tim's voice, Charlotte glanced at him. He was bent over the rat. "I don't think so." She inserted a gold earring. "Hardly anyone remembers that far back."

"If somebody's mom died when he was two, and he couldn't remember her 'cept for a picture in his room, would you think he was bad?"

"Certainly not. I can't remember a thing in my life before I broke my arm when I was four. My mother said the only reason I remember that is because everyone fussed over me so much I thought I was pretty special."

Tim slid the rat's tail through his fingers. "Snowball thinks you're special."

"Thank Snowball for me."

"You thank him." Tim dumped the small animal in her lap.

Charlotte shot a swift glance toward the half-open door. "I thought I heard your father come in."

"He's in the shower." Tim watched the small rodent climb up Charlotte's arm. "Snowball likes hiding under long hair. Sometimes I take him to school. Some of the girls hold him but most of them scream." He rolled his eyes in disgust.

"Not everyone appreciates rats." Bending over carefully so as not to dislodge the dozing rat from beneath her loose-hanging hair, Charlotte fastened her sandals.

Tim inspected her. "You going to a party?"

"No. After my bath I felt like putting on a dress for dinner." She stood up and pirouetted slowly. "How do I look?"

"Dad says you're frizlous. What's that?"

"Frivolous? It means—" just in time she caught the innocent look on Tim's face and finished awkwardly "—I don't know much about cows."

"I can tell you about them. They're big and we eat them and I like horses lots better."

"Spoken like a true cowboy." Hearing footsteps in the hall, Charlotte hastily removed Snowball from the back of her neck.

Matthew knocked perfunctorily at her open door. "Here you are," he said to his son without looking at Charlotte. "Shouldn't you be doing your chores?"

"I'm done. Smell, Dad. Doesn't it stink in here?"

Charlotte's gaze flew involuntarily to meet Matthew's. Answering amusement gleamed in his brown eyes before his gaze iced over. A second later, frostiness was replaced by wicked laughter as he saw Charlotte holding Snowball awkwardly in her hands, as far away from her as her arms would stretch. "I didn't realize you had two visitors." He propped a shoulder against the door frame. "You're quite the animal lover, aren't you?"

Charlotte gave him a baleful look. "I adore them. Tim, I think Snowball wants to go back to you." Putting on a brave smile, she added, "I don't think he likes my perfume, either."

"Go put him in his cage and wash up for dinner," Matthew said to Tim. He watched his son go down the hall to his room and then turned to Charlotte. "I thought I'd made myself clear." He shifted his stance, crossing his arms over his chest. "Leave Tim alone."

Charlotte carefully set down her comb to keep from throwing it at him. "I told your mother I'd set the table for dinner."

He blocked the doorway. "She's managed to get dinner on the table for over thirty years without your help. I expect she can manage tonight. Do we understand each other?''

"I understand you, Matthew." Reaching up slowly, Charlotte dabbed a speck of shaving cream from in front of Matthew's ear. "You think sleeping with me would be a nifty way to persuade me to sell you, on your terms, what's soon to be my ranch. However, apparently even you have some moral standards, which prevents you tomcatting around in front of your son and your mother. You're frustrated, you blame your son, and you want to punish him. You can't beat him or send him to his room, so you've decided to take away his new toy. Me. And to cast a favorable light on the matter, you're pretending you're afraid I'll harm Tim in some mysterious way." She wiped the cream off her finger onto his shirt collar. "Is there anything else I should understand?"

He grabbed her finger. "You should understand you rub me the wrong way. I don't like a woman who goes through life thinking she can get whatever she wants just by looking soft and pretty. I don't like a woman who's afraid of work because it might soil her hands or chip her nail paint. And I don't like a woman who feels sorry for herself and who thinks the world owes her because she had no father."

His contemptuous words immediately fired her anger. "For your information, Mr. Thorneton—" she jabbed him in the chest with her other finger "—I don't care one little bit whether I had a father."

"Stop poking me."

"Stop saying I feel sorry for myself. You're just jealous because Tim and I are friends."

"My son has plenty of friends." Matthew grabbed her stabbing hand. "He's looking for a mother."

"A mother," Charlotte echoed faintly.

"A mother. So I suggest, cream puff, unless you plan to become the next Mrs. Matthew Thorneton, you keep away from Tim."

"The next Mrs. Matthew..." Her hands were swallowed up by his larger ones. His hands were warm, the skin work-roughened and callused. A raw abrasion rode one knuckle. They were strong hands, yet she'd seen them pick a flower, pet a horse, tousle a small boy's hair. Those same hands had caressed his wife in their marriage bed. Had he been a gentle lover or an impatient one? Disturbed by the direction of her thoughts, Charlotte wrenched her hands from his grasp. "Don't be silly. We both know you wouldn't marry me if I owned the entire state of Colorado. I suppose threatening to marry me is another plan to scare me into hiding in my room for the entire two-week visit. I'm a necessary evil if you are to get the Gannen ranch, but that doesn't mean I'm welcome here, does it?" She glared at him. "You ought to be grateful I like Tim. If it weren't for him and your mother, you'd be out of here by now. And now, if you'll excuse me," she said pointedly as he continued to bar her way, "your mother will be wondering where I am."

He made an elaborate production of stepping aside. "I'll bet in school you were one of those little girls who thought it was feminine to flunk math." He followed her down the stairs.

"What's that supposed to mean?"

"You can't add. In your book, two and two make seven or three hundred, or anything but four."

Charlotte looked disdainfully over her shoulder at him. "If that's your clever way of calling me stupid, let me remind you, I'm not the one simple enough to think he can seduce his boss for material gain."

"That's right. You're the one who's—" his eyes gleamed at her "—toying with the hired help."

Charlotte clutched at the railing as a number of sensations swept tumultuously over her at the sight of golden-brown eyes brimming with amusement. The thought that Matthew could be dangerously attractive collided with the notion that he was laughing at her. She looked away, desperately seeking the threads of their conversation. Oh, yes, mathematics. "I was not one of those stupid girls. Aunt Faye taught me right from the start that how I did in school was based on how hard I tried, not on any worn-out gender-based stereotype."

"I'll bet you were a prim and proper little girl." He reached down and tugged on a lock of her hair. "I can picture you. Long red curls, a frilly dress, spotless white shoes and stockings. You always sat with your knees together and your hands folded in your lap."

"Naturally." The man was too stupid for words. "Pink was my favorite color, and I loved tea parties." She and Grandma Darnelle baked cookies with enthusiasm, leaving the kitchen a shambles of flour and sugar and dirty pans. "Of course, it was pretend tea because I didn't want to get my white apron dirty."

"Have you ever gotten your apron dirty, cream puff?"

"Matt, don't tease her," Helen scolded as she handed Charlotte the dinner plates. "He couldn't keep clean for two minutes. Timmy's just like him."

Tim clattered into the room. "I wanna be like Dad. He's the greatest." He grinned engagingly at his father. "Don't you think I ought to stay up later and visit with Charlotte?"

"Nope. It's a school night."

"Dad," Tim wailed. "I wanna have lots of time to bring Snowball down for Charlotte to play with."

"Tempting, very tempting," Matthew said, "but your bedtime stands. I'm sure Charlotte is exhausted after her ride this morning. She'll be turning in early, too."

That nicely hemmed her in. If she disagreed with Matthew, Tim would think she was siding with him against his father. Agreeing with Matthew meant she was allowing him to dictate her bedtime. Before she could decide how to answer, Tim demanded to know which horse she'd ridden. "Penny," she told him.

"I was right, wasn't I, Dad?" Tim asked eagerly. "They are 'zackly like."

Matthew grinned across the table. "I wouldn't say they're exactly alike."

"I should say not." Charlotte made a face at Tim. "Are you saying I look like a horse?"

"Aw, Charlotte, you know I mean your hair."

"The two of them could be peas in a pod." Matthew winked at Tim. "The only way I could tell them apart was that Penny was the one who knew what she was doing."

"I'm a born rider, and you know it."

"I admit you didn't fall off."

"What's more, I refuse to be compared to a horse."

"You're right. Comparing you to her is all wrong. Penny is the sweetest, gentlest, most even-tempered creature I've ever been around." Matthew leaned back in his chair, his mocking gaze on Charlotte. "Now a mule," he drawled, "there'd be a basis for comparison."

Helen hastily changed the subject. "Dennis said to tell you, Matt, he's planning on sending twenty-five yearlings up with you to the summer pasture."

"Who's Dennis?" Charlotte handed the butter to Tim.

"Charlie's foreman. You should have introduced him to Charlotte." Helen gave Matthew a look of reproof.

"He headed down to the south pasture long before she rolled out of bed."

"I don't know what kind of plans you've made for this place, Charlotte, but you couldn't go wrong keeping on Dennis," Helen said. "He's been working for Charlie for over twenty years. Over the years, Charlie sold off most of his land and cattle because—because of one reason or another."

"Because he had no son to leave the place to," Charlotte said precisely.

"Well, yes," Helen unhappily agreed. "Anyway, Dennis is a hard worker. Admittedly he needs some guidance now and then, but I'm sure Matt will be happy to help you there."

Charlotte wasn't thrilled with the notion forcing itself to the forefront of her mind. She glanced at Matthew. He was watching her, wickedly smug laughter in his eyes. Laughter directed at her. She forced herself to ask the question. "You don't work here, do you, Matthew?"

"No, Charlotte, actually I don't. My place runs along Charlie's land to the west."

"Why didn't you tell me?"

"You were having such a good time grinding the hapless hired hand under your heel, I didn't want to spoil your fun."

A burning flush crawled up Charlotte's face. The truth in Matthew's sardonic explanation only added to her anger and humiliation. "I suppose you have more than a house, some outbuildings and a few acres."

"Gosh, Charlotte, our ranch is one of the biggest around," a wide-eyed Tim said. "It's belonged to us Thornetons for years and years and years. Didn't you know that?"

"No, I didn't. Silly me. I had the impression your father worked for Mr. Gannen."

"I don't know where you could have gotten that idea, dear," Helen said, "although in a way, I guess you could say it's true. Matt has the power of attorney to make all the decisions and run the place until the final disposition of the estate."

"You mean he can do whatever he wants on this place," Charlotte said slowly, "and I can't."

"Naturally, cream puff, if you come to me and ask nicely, I'll consider your wishes. Oh, and Charlotte, Dennis doesn't have my easygoing personality, so don't try your tricks with him. I wouldn't be very pleased if he up and quit."

Charlotte curled her fingers in her lap. Matthew didn't even have the decency to disguise the gloating in his voice. And there was no mistaking his unspoken message. He was in charge here and he didn't want her to forget it. If it weren't for Helen and Tim, she'd kick him out on his ear. Except, she realized bitterly, she didn't have the power.

A fact that had her inwardly still seething with resentment as she sat beside Matthew in the pickup late the next morning. Outwardly she was the picture of femininity as she apologized prettily for making Matthew wait so long for her.

Matthew's only response was a grumpy acknowledgment as the pickup rattled over a cattle guard.

"I couldn't decide what a long-lost heiress should wear."

Matthew gave her a dry look before easing the pickup onto the highway. "I'm well aware your being so late was a deliberate attempt to irritate me, so don't bother to deny it."

"I wouldn't think of denying it." Charlotte tightened her seat belt with a jerk. "The liar in this truck isn't me."

"I never told you I worked for Charlie, if that's what you're referring to."

"You knew very well what I thought," she said furiously. "Not once did you bother to set me straight."

"Why should I when you were having so much fun abusing all that power you thought you had?"

"I wasn't abusing anything, and if I was—" Charlotte stared resolutely out the pickup window "—it was only because you're such an arrogant, bossy jerk."

"Me, arrogant? From the minute we met, you looked down that freckled nose at me as if I were a cow pie you'd stepped in."

"I don't like self-righteous cowboys who feel compelled to tell the rest of the world how to run their lives. You started giving me orders before we ever met. 'Go visit a man who refused to recognize your existence, Charlotte. Go fawn over a man who treated your mother like dirt. Forgive him even though he won't admit he's been wrong. Spend two weeks on the ranch. Sell the ranch to me.' Did you ever once consider my feelings? What I might want to do? No, all you cared about was what was convenient for you."

"Putting up with you is definitely not convenient."

"Too bad. What you want, Matthew Thorneton, is an ordered world. By which I mean, you giving all the orders. You want to do what you want to do, when you want to do it and how you want to do it. You didn't even have the common courtesy to ask me before you made an appointment for me in Durango today with Mr. Gannen's lawyer. Maybe I didn't want to see him today." She conveniently forgot that had been her very intention. "I pity your poor wife. You probably spent your entire married life telling her what to do and when to breathe. No doubt she died just to get away from you." The ugly remark seemed to echo endlessly in the cab of the pickup, and Charlotte was deeply ashamed of herself. Matthew's jaw was rigid. A deer standing beside the highway suddenly turned and bolted up the rocky embankment. A west-bound truck rumbled past, engine whining as it ascended into the hills. "I'm sorry," Charlotte said, stricken by her own cruelty, "my comment was inexcusable."

Matthew passed a slow-moving motor home, and then another before he spoke. "I suppose I should have checked with you before making the appointment, but I assumed you'd want the will explained to you first thing."

Her remorse evaporated. "That's your big problem. You assume too much. And mostly you assume you know better than everyone else about everything. Never mind that Charles Gannen didn't want to see me and I didn't want to see him. You decided we should meet. You assumed I would care he was dying. Why should I have? Because I'm a woman? Would you forgive someone who abandoned you?"

"If I understood, yes."

"You don't have an inkling what the word understand means."

"I sure as hell don't understand you. You were raised by a mother who's sweet and kind, and it's apparent your whole family dotes on you. But underneath that soft and frilly exterior is a core of boiling anger and hatred."

"Stick to cows and spare me your psychoanalysis. The way you behave is enough to drive a saint to a temper tantrum. After you drag me down here totally against my will, you can't expect me to be a Pollyanna about it."

"I certainly didn't expect you to bite and kick and squeal at the idea of inheriting Charlie's estate."

"What you expected, Matthew, was that you could drag me down here, dump me in your mother's lap and not have to see me again until I signed the ranch over to you two weeks later."

"Considering the red hair and the fact you're related to Charlie Gannen," he said dryly, "what I should have expected was trouble with a capital T."

"I do not have red hair."

Other than bestowing upon her an extremely derisive look, Matthew didn't bother to argue. Soon the motels and restaurants lining the highway gave notice they'd reached the outskirts of Durango. Matthew silently and competently threaded his way through the increasing traffic, his large hands resting easily on the steering wheel. Charlotte disliked the silence. Fighting with Matthew kept her thoughts from traveling down speculative and unwelcome paths. She didn't care if Chick Gannen had eaten in that restaurant, walked across that bridge or looked down at the rushing river. Wrenching her thoughts to the present, she gave a disdainful sniff. "I suppose forcing me to ride in this sorry excuse for transportation is your idea of revenge for making you late this morning."

Matthew geared down the pickup with a smooth thrust of his arm. Sunlight picked out a few hairs on the back of his tanned hand where it rested on the gearshift. "As long as I'm in town, I may as well pick up some supplies." He inspected her across the interior of the pickup. "I should have guessed a cream puff would dress for New York City or Paris, and not Durango, Colorado." Parking the pickup, he walked around to Charlotte's side of the truck and opened the door. "Here we are."

A discreet sign announced the building held the law offices of Frank Bernarde, Attorney at Law. Charlotte made a production of reading her watch. "My appointment was almost an hour ago, Matthew. After you went to all the trouble of arranging this meeting and driving me to Durango, I'm afraid Mr. Bernarde will never be able to fit me into his schedule now."

"Did I tell you your appointment was for ten this morning?" Matthew dramatically smacked his forehead. "What could I have been thinking of? Your appointment is for eleven." The look in his brown eyes was one of pure satisfaction. "And what do you know? Here we are with a couple of minutes to spare."

Charlotte's fingernails dug into her purse. In her twenty-four years of existence she'd been totally opposed to violence. Until now. Cramming that superciliously triumphant look down Matthew Thorneton's throat would give her incalculable pleasure. Ignoring his outstretched hand, she yanked open her seat belt and reached for the curb with her right foot.

Matthew caught her around the waist and swung her to the ground. "Be careful. In those shoes you're likely to break your fool neck."

"You certainly wouldn't want that, would you?" Charlotte snapped. "It might mess up your plans for acquiring my ranch."

Matthew raised an eyebrow. "Your ranch?"

"I've been helping Aunt Faye manage her store ever since I can remember. I don't think managing a ranch will be beyond my capabilities. Once it truly belongs to me and I get rid of any and all interference."

CHAPTER FIVE

MATTHEW squinted against the overhead sun as he inspected her from the top of her piled-up curls to the tips of her flimsy high-heeled sandals. "I think yesterday's horseback ride scrambled your brains."

"Not so much that I can't handle this lawyer visit on my own." He was too close to her, crowding her, but she refused to step back. He seemed to have forgotten his hands were resting warmly on her waist. "Don't think you can horn in and dominate the conversation. There are things I want to know, and I intend to know them. If I have to stay there all day."

"If that's the way you feel, I won't go in at all."

His capitulation came too easily. Charlotte frowned at him. "Why not?"

He crossed his arms across his chest and leaned against the pickup, one booted foot propped up on the curb. "You are the most contentious and illogical woman I've ever met. First you accuse me of never consulting you, and then, when I do go along with your expressed wishes, you immediately suspect my motives."

"Maybe because from the moment you walked into the shop, you've done nothing but coerce and manipulate me."

"I wouldn't have to do either if you would listen to reason at least once in awhile."

"If you ever said anything reasonable, I might listen."

Matthew gave her a disgusted look. "You're going to be late for your appointment if you don't get in there." Straightening, he pointed to a large brick building in view above the rooftops. "That's the Strater Hotel. I'll meet you there for lunch in two hours."

"I don't want to eat there," Charlotte said instantly.

"The Strater's an institution in this town—" Matthew rammed his wide-brimmed hat lower over his forehead "—and you're eating there."

"I'm not."

"If I have to tear this town apart looking for you, wrestle you to the ground, hog-tie you, haul you in there over my shoulder and tie you to a chair, you are going to eat lunch at the Strater," he said distinctly. "In two hours."

Charlotte spun around and flounced up the walk to the heavily carved front door of the law office.

Two and a half hours later she ambled down Main Avenue, pausing occasionally to inspect the contents of store windows. An intricate silver and turquoise necklace caught her eye, and she stopped again. The Strater Hotel was one block farther down the street. No doubt Matthew Thorneton was complacently sitting there at this very minute in full expectation Charlotte would dutifully eat lunch with him. As ordered.

Thinking about him made Charlotte's teeth ache. Not only was he bossy and overbearing, he was a sneaky, underhanded thief. And insulting. His allowing her to see Mr. Bernarde alone spoke volumes about Matthew Thorneton's arrogant self-confidence. It also clearly indicated he thought Charlotte too stupid to understand the significance and ramifications of the old man's will.

A noisy growl came from the region of her stomach, and she glanced at her watch. It was after one-thirty, surely late enough to have made her point that no devious, blowhard cowboy should count on having things his way.

Entering the imposing hotel through glass and carved wood double doors, it suddenly occurred to Charlotte Matthew was the type to head back to the ranch without her to teach her a lesson. She paused uncertainly at the entrance to the dining room. Matthew Thorneton was nowhere in sight.

"Looking for someone, cream puff?"

Charlotte started at the voice in her ear. "Certainly not."

"I was in the lobby waiting for you." His hand in the middle of her back, Matthew directed her to a corner table by the windows in the elegant dining room. As she settled into the trim, fabric-covered armchair he pulled out for her, he added, "I'm glad to see you haven't been cooped up in a stuffy law office all this time."

Charlotte stowed the large quantity of parcels beneath her chair and accepted a menu from the waitress. "That business took less than thirty minutes." The lawyer had shown her the will, commented on its unusual nature, given her a list of what the estate contained and answered her questions. "I spent the rest of the morning shopping for presents to take home."

"And killing time," he said with an amused gleam in his eyes as the waitress returned. When the woman departed with their orders, Matthew leaned back in his chair and sipped his water, studying her over the rim of his glass. "I wasn't expecting you this early. I thought sure you'd hold out at least until two."

Charlotte ignored the provocative remark and surveyed the dining room decor. Stained glass, a crystal chandelier hanging from the high ceiling and green walls with pink molded swags bespoke the elegance of a previous century.

Matthew echoed her thoughts. "The hotel was built back in the 1880s. About the same time an ancestor of mine filed claim to our place."

"He'd certainly be surprised to see the ranch today. Especially the way it's grown over the past ten years."

Matthew had no trouble interpreting her words. "Charlie wanted to sell and I was willing to buy," he said evenly.

"Willing to buy. How generous of you that sounds. Don't you mean eager to buy at bargain-basement prices?"

"Frank Bernarde didn't tell you that."

"Certainly not. He was quick to assure me Charles Gannen was quite satisfied with the conditions of sale."

"But you're not." It wasn't a question. When Charlotte failed to respond, Matthew said in an exasperated voice, "Charlie was the shrewdest horse trader around."

Charlotte gave the waitress a quick smile of thanks and dipped her fork into the fruit salad the woman set before her.

"But we aren't talking just about horses, are we? We're talking about land and cows and all kinds of stuff. As far as I can figure out, Charles Gannen sold you about everything but mineral rights, water rights and the kitchen sink." She pointed a fork loaded with watermelon at Matthew. "I think you took advantage of an old man who held no hope for the future."

Matthew raised a mocking brow. "Since when have you been Charlie's champion?"

"If he went barefoot because you cheated him out of the boots on his feet, I couldn't care less. Just don't think I'm as easy a mark. If I decide to sell to you, I'll..." Charlotte totally forgot what she was going to say as she spotted the blond woman standing at the entrance to the dining room. Charlotte recognized the woman instantly. The previous evening she'd seen the woman's portrait sitting beside Tim's bed.

"You'll what?" Matthew prompted before realizing Charlotte was looking past him. He swiveled in his chair, and stiffened.

The woman walking toward them was blond and blue-eyed. She was a beauty, if one ignored the small lines of discontent etched in her face, lines that would give her a fretful appearance as she aged. The black of her form-fitting shirt should have been wrong for her, but it made her look sexy and sophisticated. Long silver and turquoise earrings dangled to her shoulders, silver cuffs ringed both her wrists, and colorful stones decorated the woman's fingers as she curved her hand around the back of Matthew's neck. "Matt, darling, I thought I saw your disreputable pickup parked down the street."

"Paula." Matthew rose slowly to his feet. "I hadn't heard you were back."

The blond woman's sleek eyebrows rose skyward. "Darling, I can see that. Aren't you going to introduce your new—" she paused infinitesimally "—friend?"

"Charlotte," Matthew said in studied politeness, "this is Paula Kenton, my wife Lara's younger sister. Paula, I'd like you to meet Charlotte Darnelle."

His voice left not the slightest doubt in Charlotte's mind that as much as Matthew disliked her, he disliked Paula Kenton even more. Charlotte immediately invited her to join them.

Matthew gave Charlotte a dark look. "Take my chair, Paula. I'll get another."

The next few minutes Charlotte ate her salad as Paula organized her possessions, the waitress and their seating arrangements. Charlotte was not surprised when Paula refused Matthew's chair and settled firmly into a chair between Matthew and Charlotte. Paula was obviously taking no chances on anyone taking her sister's place. Anyone else, Charlotte corrected herself, covertly studying Paula as the other woman chatted vivaciously with Matthew, her head close to his, her hand resting on his forearm.

The woman's conversation centered on people and events Charlotte could have no knowledge of, by design, Charlotte felt sure. Her attention wandered to her surroundings. Outside, a sparrow hopped off the curb in pursuit of an elusive crumb. Tourists wandered by eating ice-cream cones. A couple hesitated outside the window and peered inside at the dining room's interior. Most of the tables were empty now. Several hikers, their backpacks at their feet, laughed at one table while two suit-clad business men conversed quietly at another.

"Have you recently moved to Durango, Charlene?" The blond beauty deigned to notice Charlotte.

Charlotte set down her elegant stemmed water glass. "No. I'm—"

"Staying with us," Matthew smoothly interjected, at the same time unleashing a warm smile across the table in Charlotte's direction. "Charlotte might decide to live around here—" his eyelids drooped sensually "—permanently."

If Charlotte hadn't already swallowed her water, she'd have choked to death. Matthew's statement intimated there was something between them. She opened her mouth to deny any such possibility. "Ouch."

"I'm sorry, Charlotte. Did I kick you? There's not much leg room under this table. You were saying?"

Charlotte bared her teeth at him. "I was saying, Matthew, that—"

"Matthew? You let her call you Matthew?"

A slow smile crawled across his face. "I like the prissy little voice she says it in."

Before Charlotte could tell Matthew to take a flying leap off a tall building, Paula asked, "Since when have you liked prissy women, Matt? I thought your taste ran to women who could string fence, jockey a tractor and ride fast and hard."

"Riding fast and hard is your preference, not mine," Matthew said. "Don't let those frilly clothes fool you. Charlotte is a born rider, isn't that right, Charlotte?"

He'd boxed her in, and the amusement in his eyes told Charlotte he was well aware of it. She wasn't about to confess to a sneering Paula that Matthew considered her as suitable to ranch living as an orchid was to living in Antarctica. On the other hand, if Paula was a threat to Matthew's bachelor status, he could look for another poor female to hide behind. Charlotte didn't appreciate being thrown as fresh meat in front of the predatory Paula. She opted for what she hoped would be middle ground. "I certainly enjoyed riding Penny."

"You let her ride Penny when you won't let me ride her?"

"I told you years ago you'd never ride another horse of mine. I haven't changed my mind."

"You spoil your animals," Paula said petulantly. "I suppose your son is still hauling around that filthy vermin-ridden rodent. That creature is not to come to my house while I'm there, or I'll turn it loose in the barn for the cats."

Charlotte looked at the pink tablecloth, not trusting herself to speak. Matthew abruptly pushed back his chair and rose. "Let's go, Charlotte. We have another stop to make."

Paula stood up and threw her arms around his neck. "All right, you old meanie, I won't say another word about your precious son. Call me. Mom and Dad would like to see you.''

He loosened her arms. "I saw them the other day."

She ran her fingers across his shoulders. "I haven't seen Helen for ages."

"I'll tell her you're back. Ready, Charlotte?"

Charlotte scrambled to her feet. "If you are, Matthew." Smiling determinedly at him as he clasped her elbow, she hoped her voice sounded suitably prissy.

"I'll be damned." Paula stared at Charlotte's shoes. "Where did Matt find you, anyway?"

"Denver."

"I think you'd better run right back there," Paula said. "You and Matt wouldn't last together five minutes. You're the weak, silly, romantic type, and Matt needs a woman who's strong and tough. Ranch living isn't all it's cracked up to be, Charlene. If you don't believe me, ask Matt why my sister left him." Paula turned to Matthew and laid her long fingers against his cheek. "Not that I care about that." Standing on tiptoes, she pressed her mouth against Matthew's thinned lips. "Call me," she ordered throatily, running her nails down the side of his face. Then she whirled and was gone.

Leaving behind an awkward silence. Charlotte rubbed her elbow. Matthew had gripped it so hard at his sister-in-law's words, it was a wonder any feeling remained. "I didn't know it was possible to flounce in cowboy boots. Or even to walk in jeans that tight." Not for a million dollars would she ask for an explanation of Paula's remark about her sister. Nor would she comment on the faint white streaks running down Matthew's face. And, as he dragged her through the hotel lobby, she certainly didn't think it prudent to ask him to repeat whatever it was he'd growled half under his breath.

Matthew barely allowed Charlotte time to belt herself in the pickup before throwing the truck into gear and charging into traffic. "Thanks," he snarled.

"For letting your sister-in-law assume we're a cozy twosome?" Another savage shift thrust her against the seat.

"I fully expected you to declare you'd rather date Snowball than me." He spared her a quick glance. "Why didn't you?"

"She irritated me."

Matthew snorted. "An attractive woman always brings out Paula's claws. Pay no attention to her."

The compliment was sweeter by virtue of being unintentional. Never mind Matthew's conclusion was off one hundred and eighty degrees. Paula's attitude toward Tim was the sole reason Charlotte hadn't set her straight. Hating the idea of the woman as Tim's next mother, Charlotte decided to subtly probe. "Paula certainly looks like the picture Tim has of his mother."

"Next to my wife, Paula is a flawed imitation," he said curtly. "Lara was beautiful and charming, the perfect, dutiful daughter. Everything came easily to her. Paula wanted everything Lara had, and never quite understood why she always came up short. She's the black sheep of her family, twenty-eight years old and never settled to anything, including a husband. She's been married and divorced three times."

The pickup sped across a bridge spanning the Animas River. Below them two kayaks and a large rubber raft bobbed on the turbulent waters. "Maybe the man she wanted was unavailable."

"I wondered when you'd get around to that remark of Paula's about Lara leaving me." Matthew swung the truck around a sharp curve and headed up a steep hill.

"I thought your wife was dead."

"She is." He shifted with a harsh clash of gears. "We were temporarily living apart—working out some problems."

Hearing the pain in his voice, Charlotte glanced quickly at him. His jaw might have been chiseled from granite. Uncertain how to respond, she looked out the window. They'd ascended a steep hill, and Durango was spread out below. Ahead of them was a large, well-kept cemetery. Cold foreboding swept over Charlotte. Surely he didn't expect... "If you think I'm the least bit interested in where Charles Gannen is buried, you're wrong. Unless you thought I might want to dance on his grave."

Matthew parked the pickup. "Your grandmother, Emily Gannen, is here, too. Next to your dad."

"You mean Chick Gannen?" Matthew couldn't make her look. Not at gravestones. The sky was an empty, faded blue-gray. Two crows flew by, their feathers funereal black.

"Didn't you know he was buried here?"

"No."

"I can show you where his—"

"No." The irritating noise of a tractor mowing grass came from the other side of the cemetery.

Matthew gave her a long, thoughtful look, tapping the fingers of one hand on the steering wheel. Finally he said, "My family and the Gannens go way back. I was a kid when Chick left. Believe it or not, your dad used to baby-sit me. He was a happy-go-lucky cowpoke." Amusement crept into his voice. "You didn't get your temper from him."

"I don't have a temper."

He didn't bother to refute her tight-lipped statement. "I thought your dad could do no wrong." Leaning back, Matthew tipped his hat forward over his eyes. "When it came to riding or throwing a loop, Chick was the best, and I wanted to grow up to be just like him.''

Charlotte carefully pleated her skirt fabric between two fingers. Everyone had memories of Chick Gannen. ''Your maudlin stories of the past don't interest me, nor does this place, so we can leave any time.'' She was proud of her calm, steady voice.

Matthew straightened slowly, pushing back his hat. ''My mistake.'' Reaching down to start the engine, he hesitated, his fingers hovering over the keys in the ignition. With a sudden decisive move, he grabbed the keys and yanked them free. ''I need some fresh air. I'll be back in a minute.'' He stepped out of the pickup, closing the door quietly behind him.

Mustn't wake the dead, Charlotte thought crazily, her gaze focused on her hands in her lap. Odd hands, with white knuckles next to pink fingers she was squeezing together too tightly. Relax, she told herself. Think of something pleasant. Christmas presents. Surprises. Shopping in downtown Denver. She'd always loved that. The tiny element of hope... No, she wouldn't think of that. She'd think of flowers. No, not flowers, not here. Her childhood. That was safe. She'd been a silly child. Walking downtown streets or at the airport or in any crowded place, scrutinizing the faces of all the men passing by. The lump in her throat grew painfully large. All those years of pretending that somewhere she had an actual, living father. Only she hadn't. Never, ever. The man who'd fathered her was, and had been, nothing more than a pile of bleached bones.

The dashboard in front of her blurred. Never would a strange man walking down the street see her and cry out she looked so much like someone in his family she must be his daughter. Charlotte brushed the moisture from one cheek. Years ago she'd told herself firmly she had no father and her fantasy of running into him on the street was no more than that—a fantasy. Unfortunately, deep in her heart, she'd never discarded the dream. Coming here had been a tragic mistake. Never again could she pretend, even to herself, that the man who'd fathered her walked the streets of Durango.

Chick Gannen was dead. Dead and buried, and had been since before her birth. If she climbed from the truck she could walk to his headstone and read the engraved proof. Not that she needed to read it to know what it would say. She squeezed her eyelids tightly shut. Charles Gannen, Jr. Killed in action.

Left unwritten would be that he'd been mourned separately by his parents and the woman who'd loved him well, if not wisely. No mention would be made of his child. The child he'd never known. The child who would never know him. Because he wasn't a person. He was a moldering body in a casket. Measured footsteps approached the other side of the pickup, and Charlotte quickly turned her back to Matthew.

He opened his door and slid beneath the steering wheel. "I apologize for dragging you here." His voice rang, not with contrition, but with anger. "I thought you'd be interested in where your father is buried."

"You were wrong." Charlotte forced the words between trembling lips and fumbled with her purse. Why did the stupid zipper have to stick now, of all times? Intent on her task, she failed to see the hand reaching across the wide seat. Grasping her chin firmly, Matthew turned her head toward him. With his other hand he removed the large golden straw hat, which shielded her face. Charlotte blinked rapidly in a futile attempt to stem the flow of tears down her cheeks and stared blindly at Matthew's middle shirt button. "Why aren't we leaving?"

Pulling a white handkerchief from his jeans pocket, he handed it to her. "Use this before your freckles float away."

Charlotte jerked her chin out of Matthew's grasp and turned her back solidly to him before blowing her nose hard. Maybe she needed the handkerchief, but she didn't need pity. "It's the pollen from the pine trees." Salty moisture continued to well up and spill over from traitorous eyes, and she scrubbed her cheeks with the back of her hand. The car springs bounced slightly as Matthew slid to the middle of the seat. She could feel the heat from his body, feel him studying her. Like a bug under a microscope. She hunched her shoulders, rejecting any overtures of sympathy before he could make them.

"Odd it didn't bother you yesterday when we were riding."

"Allergies come on suddenly," she choked out, jumping as his large hands came down on her shoulders.

Matthew's fingers pressed against her tense shoulders, his thumbs drawing wide circles on either side of her rigid spine. "Want to talk about it?"

"No." The handkerchief muffled her voice as she blew her nose again. The hard pads of Matthew's thumbs relentlessly kneaded her flesh. "There's nothing to talk about."

"I'm surprised you and your mom haven't visited the cemetery before. It shouldn't have been hard to figure out where Chick was buried."

Among the pine and willow branches a slight breeze droned a funeral dirge. "Charles Gannen told my mother—" she hiccuped "—he was in a helicopter that was shot down."

"He was." Matthew continued to rub her tense back muscles.

"At sea." Documentaries on sharks gave her nightmares. "He said they'd never recovered the bodies."

Matthew's fingers stilled. "Charlie went a little crazy when Chick died."

His fingers were hard pokers digging painfully deep in her shoulders. "Don't you dare defend him." Her tears finally ceased to flow, and Charlotte mopped her face with the wadded-up handkerchief. "He was a mean, cruel man."

Matthew resumed his measured massage. "Charlie Gannen was quick-tempered and could carry a grudge longer than anyone I know, but he was fair and generous. He was the first to show up when a friend had troubles. If it hadn't been for Charlie, Mom and I couldn't have managed when Dad died. Charlie did things I don't agree with, but he was a good friend."

"That certainly says something about you, doesn't it?" The air in the pickup suffocated her. Charlotte scrambled out, escaping Matthew's touch. She inhaled deep pine-scented breaths.

"Do you want your hat?" Matthew held it out as he stood beside her.

She shook her head. In front of her a rosy pink granite tombstone spoke of the death, decades earlier, of a young woman, wife and mother of two children. "She died too young," Charlotte said abruptly. "Her poor husband, left with two babies. How could he manage?"

"He didn't manage. He survived. At first, he'd be numb. Later would come the rage, cursing the fates, wild rides at midnight while the children were sleeping." Matthew shoved his hands into his pockets and stared off into the distance. "Finally would come, not acceptance, but a kind of resignation and the realization that life must go on. For the children."

Matthew's clipped words penetrated Charlotte's fog of self-pity. He was talking about himself. She pushed a small pebble with the toe of her shoe. "It must have been horrible for you when your wife died. Tim said he was only two." She hesitated. "Is she here? Is that where you went a minute ago?"

"Yes."

"Did you see her dead? Her body?"

"Yes."

"At least you knew." A few feet away newly laid sod gave evidence of a recent grave. Charlotte stared blindly at it. "I used to imagine ways Chick Gannen might have survived. I even prayed he was a prisoner over there. One of those who wasn't sent back. Wishing that kind of hell on him because I wanted someday for him to come back. Not for Mom, but for me." She twisted the sodden handkerchief. "You don't have to tell me how sick and selfish that is." Fresh tears welled in her eyes.

"Death is hell on the ones left behind." Reaching out, Matthew took her hand and led her to a trio of simple blue-gray headstones. "Emily planted the first bulbs, and Mom took over after Emily died. She'll add some this fall for Charlie."

A dozen bearded iris grew between two of the stones, their huge sunshine-yellow blossoms thrusting toward the sky. She touched one with the tip of a finger. The steel gray granite drew her nearer. The stone was cool and polished against her palm. Almost to herself she said, "Years ago my mother planted lavender iris in our backyard. She plans to dig them up and divide them this year." Charlotte traced the name, the chiseled indentations catching at the skin of her finger. Matthew stood at the edge of her vision. "We planted crocuses and daffodils on Grandpa Darnelle's grave. Last year it snowed when they bloomed and I worried they'd die, but they didn't.'' She ran her palm back and forth over the top of the stone. ''Where he is, there are Canada geese everywhere. Aunt Faye says signs of life in a cemetery speak well of the rhythms of nature.''

''She'll like this place.'' Matthew pointed to a spot about thirty feet in front of them. A golden-mantled ground squirrel perched on top of a pale gray gravestone. Two smaller ones chased each other around the base of the stone.

Charlotte would return with her camera to take pictures for her mother. Chick Gannen's final resting place would please Jewel. Many of the graves were decorated with flowers—plants, cut flowers in containers or artificial flowers. Trees of various types, sizes and colors dotted the hillside, and not far away grew a large peony bush covered with deep rose-colored blooms. The cemetery was on a hilltop, but even higher hills rose in the distance. A flicker flew past with a rush of wings and a flash of russet, and a chickadee called from a tall pine. Bright green aspen leaves danced in the slight June breeze. Even the weeds were bright and cheery, yellow dandelions and pale pink clover blossoms winding through the green grass. The haunting cry of a train whistle drifted up from the valley.

Matthew stirred at her side. ''Lara loved train whistles.''

''You loved her,'' Charlotte said in some surprise.

''Yes.'' He turned to trace his steps to the pickup.

Charlotte followed him. His simple reply spoke volumes. After Paula's insinuations, Charlotte had pictured a marriage damaged beyond repair. The feeling in Matthew's voice contradicted that picture. Since arriving at the Gannen place Charlotte had wondered why Matthew lived with his mother instead of taking a second wife. His first wife had been dead six years, and there must be plenty of women willing to take on another woman's son, a rat and an arrogant cowboy. Especially when that cowboy came with obvious virility, more than passable looks and the old family ranch. If Matthew put an ad in the paper he'd have applicants lining up.

Charlotte clicked her seat belt fastened. Many people would consider six years plenty long to mourn. They wouldn't understand why Matthew didn't remarry, embarking upon a second journey through wedded bliss. Charlotte wasn't most people. Chick Gannen had been killed in Vietnam, and Jewel Darnelle had been faithful to his memory for the past twenty-five years. Jewel's parents had celebrated over forty years of marriage before death parted them. Charlotte had never heard the details, but she knew even Aunt Faye was part of the Darnelle tradition of constancy, having fought with her fiancé on the eve of their marriage, and then remained single when he'd married someone else on the rebound. For some people a single, abiding love nourished them for a lifetime. They wanted no second love. Paula Kenton was wasting her time if she expected Matthew to present her with wedding ring number four.

Not that Matthew didn't deserve Paula. The memory of her conversation with Frank Bernarde tightened Charlotte's jaw. The visit to the lawyer's office went a long way toward explaining Matthew's bouts of flirtatious behavior. He must think she was a complete imbecile. Even his behavior at the cemetery looked less kind and more calculated when viewed through informed eyes. Oh, yes, Matthew Thorneton thought Charlotte was easy prey, a silly weak female he could manipulate at will. As no doubt those tight jeans and golden-brown eyes had been manipulating women since his birth. From the minute she'd stepped foot on the Gannen ranch, she'd suspected Matthew wanted something. Now she knew exactly what that something was. He'd told Paula he liked the prissy way Charlotte said his name. That wasn't what he liked about Charlotte, at all. She gave him a disarming smile.

He smiled back, his right hand on the gear shift. "How's your ankle?"

"Where you kicked me? I'll probably barely be able to hobble tomorrow. It's a wonder you didn't break it. We weak, prissy women have very delicate bones, you know."

Matthew's gaze roamed over her from head to toe. "At times I get the oddest feeling you're not nearly as delicate as you look, cream puff. In spite of those ruffles and lace."

"You're right, Matthew." She fluttered her eyelashes at him. "I'm sure I could twine fences and ride horses every bit as fast as your sister-in-law."

Matthew's mouth twitched. "I think you mean string fence."

"Whatever. The point is, I'm sure the only difference between me and Paula Kenton, besides our choice of clothing, is my prissy little voice. Matthew," she added prissily.

His laughter was low and intimate. "I wonder how prissy you'd be in a man's bed. If a man stripped you of your ruffles and lace, would he strip you of your prissy ways, too? I suspect, cream puff, lying in a man's bed, wearing nothing but cream-colored flesh and freckles, your red hair foaming over the pillow, you wouldn't have an ounce of prissiness in you."

Heat flamed through Charlotte's veins at the sexual awareness gleaming deep in brown eyes. "I'm a straw-berry-blond," she said automatically, her gaze glued to his lips, her mind running riot at the thought of those lips pressed against hers. Those lips curved in satisfaction. Arrogant, male, triumphant satisfaction. Smoldering anger drove every other emotion from her body. Except one. Reluctant admiration. Matthew Thorneton was good. Very good.

"I think I could grow extremely fond of strawberries," he murmured. "Strawberries and cream."

Charlotte curved her lips in a smile that matched his centimeter for insincere centimeter. "Do you?" she purred. "And do you think you could grow as fond of my other little attributes and assets? Such as—water rights?"

CHAPTER SIX

"WATER rights?" he asked.

As if she'd spoken in a foreign tongue. As if the words meant nothing to him. "You know. Water rights. Those things Charles Gannen leased to you but refused to sell. The same water rights I'm going to own in two weeks. When you were singing your sad song of wanting to buy this ranch for your dear ol' mom, you somehow neglected to mention those little ol' water rights."

"I saw no point in complicating things." A small flock of sparrows scattered in panic before the speeding truck as Matthew drove out of Durango, headed to the ranch.

"Unfortunately for you, your lawyer friend didn't realize I'm supposed to be simpleminded. Even worse for you, good ol' Frank took one look at me and mistook me for someone with a bleeding heart. He was at great pains to point out without that water you've been leasing, that little ol' land you bought from Charles Gannen wouldn't be worth the little ol' weeds growing on it. Goodness gracious, those little ol' water rights seem to be worth a mint to you. That's not too complicated to understand, even for little ol' me."

"If you say *little ol'* one more time, I'm going to wring your neck."

"I don't think so, Matthew, because you sure don't want those water rights falling into the hands of Connie what's her name. Your friend Frank explained how she married some hotshot California businessman who's somebody big in a water consortium. What do you think the chances are Connie would sell you those water rights?'' Charlotte studied Matthew's tanned, weathered profile. Squint lines radiated from the corner of his eye, a muscle twitched along his granite jaw, and a deep frown creased his forehead. "Pretty slim," she answered her own question. "I suspect you'd be up a creek without a paddle. Or water."

"Charlie intended for me to have those water rights."

"So your friend Frank said, only, gosh darn, somehow Charles Gannen never got around to selling them to you. Or maybe he did offer to sell, and you were holding out until he died because you thought he'd will them to your mother. In which case, those water rights wouldn't have cost you a single penny."

Matthew's hands tightened on the steering wheel. "Charlie was born and bred on this land. He knew water was its life blood, and letting go of one drop of water was anathema to him whether he needed that water or not. It's no secret his previous wills left the water rights to me, free and clear. He knew what that water meant to me. Once he got off his high horse, he'd have been reasonable."

"Most people wouldn't consider leaving an estate to one's only granddaughter unreasonable," Charlotte said sweetly.

Matthew snorted. "Charlie wasn't thinking about reasonable when he willed everything to you. He was thinking about teaching Mom a lesson. She told him in no uncertain terms her opinion of his treatment of you and your mother. Charlie didn't like having his behavior questioned, especially when he knew he was wrong. I think, deep down, Charlie regretted cutting himself off from his only grandchild, but backing down was impossible for him. If you'd come as I asked you—"

"Ordered."

"—all this could have been settled."

"Giving you the water rights."

Matthew heaved a long-suffering sigh. "Charlie built his ranch up from nothing, and it weighed heavily on him he had no descendants. Frank said Charlie showed up with the will giving you the ranch, handwritten and obviously added to and changed over time. Almost if he'd been secretly nourishing the possibility you'd come here, fall in love with the place and want to stay. A Gannen on Gannen land. Mom and I think that's why Charlie put in the two-week-visit stipulation. Charlie had the will laying around when he got mad at Mom, so he used it."

"I'm not a Gannen and he never wanted me here. He just liked the idea of forcing me to do something I'd hate."

"After Charlie met you, he would have seen his will treated you fairly. He wouldn't have left you out."

"Not having met me, he didn't leave me out." She'd never seen anyone gnash his teeth before. "He left you out."

The now-familiar silhouette of the Sleeping Ute lay on the horizon before Matthew spoke again. "Once Charlie thought Mom had learned her lesson, he'd have gone back to Frank's and pulled that will. It was bad luck he died before he could. He wanted me to have those water rights."

"So everyone keeps telling me. Maybe he did." Charlotte smoothed her dress over her knees. "But that's hardly incentive for me to sell them to you, is it? Especially after the way you intended to cheat me."

"I never made a secret of the fact I wanted Charlie's ranch and all that went with it," he said with exaggerated patience. "No one's trying to cheat you. I intend to pay fair value for the land, the house and the water.

You might remember who set up the appointment for you with Frank."

"I'm curious, Matthew. Did you think your friend Frank would gloss over those water rights, and I'd be too stupid to notice, or did you ask him to appeal to my generous nature?"

"Well, gee, Charlotte, it would hardly be the latter, would it? Since I know damned well you don't have a generous nature."

"You did think I was too stupid to catch on. How unfortunate for you Mr. Bernarde seems to possess some integrity and refused to go along with your petty scheming."

"There was no scheming," he bit out. "I didn't even talk to Frank. I made your appointment through his secretary and merely told Alice you wanted to see the will."

"Because you'd already given Mr. Bernarde his instructions." They turned onto the dirt road. "Did you give him those instructions before or after you went to Denver?"

"Damn it, Charlotte, there were no instructions." The pickup bumped violently over a cattle guard.

She waited until they'd almost reached the ranch house. "That was such a touching story you told about your poor, homeless mother."

"I never said she was homeless," he snapped. "Charlie never intended that damned will to be his final one, but since it was, he might as well have slapped my mother's face in public. You ought to be able to understand that."

"You mean I ought to be able to understand rejection and injustice. I certainly do, Matthew. I also understand when someone is using my past in an attempt to manipulate me. Did it ever occur to you to tell me the truth?"

Matthew pulled up in front of the house and turned to face Charlotte. "I went up to Denver with every intention of laying all my cards on the table and working out a fair business deal with you. Only you made it crystal clear you intended to be every bit as obstructive and contrary as your grandfather was.''

''Do not compare me to Charles Gannen.''

''Impossible not to. When it comes to illogical, stubborn and cantankerous behavior, you and Charlie are carbon copies of each other. Charlie was mad at himself and took it out on Mom. You're mad at Charlie, only he's beyond your reach, so you're taking your anger out on me.'' He snorted in disgust. ''Two minutes of dealing with you, and Charlie would have known you were his granddaughter. You're every bit as proficient as he was at cutting your nose off to spite your face.''

''If you want to advance your cause, Matthew, name-calling and yelling at me is hardly the way to go about it.'' She let a half minute tick by. ''There are better ways to influence me.''

''I see,'' Matthew said grimly. ''How much?''

''Money isn't everything.'' A kestrel hovered overhead, searching for prey.

''Quit playing games, Charlotte. What do you want?''

''A number of different things have occurred to me.''

''I'll bet.''

Charlotte smiled and uncrossed her legs. Even when bringing a man like Matthew Thorneton to his knees, one could still behave as a lady.

''School's out! School's out!'' Tim careened through the front door. ''Where's Dad?''

''Over at his place,'' Helen said.

''Oh.'' Tim dug the toe of his shoe into the rug. ''I thought him and me could do something with Charlotte.''

"Penny's still here," Helen said. "Why don't you and Charlotte ride over and surprise your dad?"

Considering Matthew had told her in no uncertain terms to keep away from Tim, it certainly would be a surprise, Charlotte thought, attempting to discourage the idea. Her objections were overruled, and before she could invent an acceptable excuse not to go, Helen had phoned down to the barn with instructions to saddle the horses and Tim had devoured his after-school snack and was waiting impatiently for Charlotte.

Tim's reception of her riding outfit was bluntly to the point. He was still giggling as they rode through the pastures between the two ranches. Less than a mile as the crow flies, Helen had assured Charlotte. Neither Tim nor his grandmother expressed a moment's doubt as to Charlotte's ability to make the ride, apparently having taken Charlotte at her word that she was a born rider. The one thing Charlotte was sure she needn't worry about was Matthew's opinion of her riding skills being swayed by anything Tim said.

The late-afternoon sun sparkled off the snowy peaks of the San Juans, and small white-blossomed lilies waved at the slightest breeze. Moving in and out of the cottonwood shadows beside the rushing stream, the horses flushed red-winged blackbirds into the sky. Signs of new life abounded. Across the road two colts gamboled in the field, their mothers placidly grazing nearby. In a small pond fluffy gray Canada goslings swam swiftly to their mothers' sides. Big-eyed calves ran snorting in pretend panic to their mothers as Charlotte and Tim rode by.

Charlotte's enjoyment of the ride was blunted by apprehension about their destination. More accurately, what was going to happen at their destination. She and Matthew had not exactly parted on friendly terms earlier this afternoon. He'd neither accepted her ultimatum nor rejected it. What he had done was give her a look of absolute outrage, erupt from the truck slamming the door behind him and stomp down to the barn. She hadn't laid eyes on him since. Since he was bound to leap to the erroneous conclusion that there was a connection between the water rights issue and her showing up with Tim, Matthew's mood was not likely to improve.

Matthew's pickup was parked in the shade of a tall blue spruce. Charlotte reined Penny in beside a split rail fence. Beyond a wide expanse of dandelion-decorated lawn sat a dignified old farmhouse. Two stories high, the white-framed house sported black shutters and a barn-red door. A lilac bush in the last stages of bloom showered the ground with lavender petals. Poppies blazed orange along the fence. Dismounting, Charlotte put Penny's reins in Tim's outstretched hand. Waiting until he'd secured the horses in the shade along the fence, she followed him into the house.

Tim's yells failed to turn up his dad. "I'll see if he's down at the barn. You can wait here."

Standing in the front hall, Charlotte cravenly agreed. Let Tim break the news of his visitor to his father. Matthew wasn't likely to erupt in front of his son, and by the time he reached the house, he might have his temper under control. A half smile played across her mouth. It would be interesting to see if Matthew succumbed to what he referred to as cutting one's nose off to spite his face. It was not in his best interest to alienate Charlotte right now.

She looked around. Even furnished, the house had that stale air of abandonment peculiar to vacant houses. Ahead a staircase climbed to the upper regions of the house. To the left of the stairs, a hallway led to the back of the house. On either side of the entry, partially closed doors beckoned. Charlotte peeked into the room on her right. It was a beige living room, stiff and formal. In the room across the hall, the drapes were closed, but low-riding, western rays seeped through the thin fabric providing enough light to see the room was furnished with cast-offs and cluttered with knickknacks. Charlotte stepped inside. Faded pillows and hand-knit afghans were stacked and neatly folded. Glass doors on the fireplace were closed, the fireplace swept, the log holder empty. A television screen stared blankly. The room was spotlessly clean and void of life.

Charlotte slowly swiveled. A large black piano graced one corner of the room, a collection of framed photographs on the closed lid. A likeness of Chick Gannen drew her. He held a younger version of Tim—Matthew at about four years of age, she guessed. They appeared to be at a picnic. Helen was in the picture with her first husband, his arm draped over Helen's shoulders. Matthew had inherited his father's build, the wide shoulders, strong thighs and long legs. Charlotte studied the kind eyes and laughing mouth of the man in the photo. There was strength in his face, and he radiated the same sense of self-assurance that characterized Matthew. Matthew wore that same look of pride and pleasure when he looked at Tim. Whatever else she thought about Matthew, he was a good father. She set down the picture, her gaze moving on. The photo of a baby in his mother's arms was obviously Tim and Matthew's wife. What had he called her? Lara. Charlotte studied the picture, seeing now how Lara and Paula only superficially resembled each other. Lara, with her cloud of hair so blond it was almost white, glowed with an inner radiance and feminine beauty. Paula would look hard and coarse beside Lara. Charlotte felt a stab of pity for Matthew's sister-in-law.

Reaching for a wedding portrait of Matthew and Lara, Charlotte marveled at how young they looked. How beautiful. The look on Matthew's face as he gazed at his young bride was a mixture of happiness, possessiveness, satisfaction and anticipation. Matthew was looking forward to the joys of his marital bed. Unexpected sharp envy pierced Charlotte's insides, and she set the picture down with a thump. An inlaid wood frame held another photograph of Matthew's deceased wife. Even in jeans and faded plaid shirt, Lara was gorgeous. Her engaging wide smile and white perfect teeth belonged in a toothpaste advertisement. She sat her horse with a born-in-the-saddle ease Charlotte envied. Lara must have been the perfect wife for Matthew. No wonder he'd loved her too much to ever replace her.

"What are you doing here?"

Charlotte whirled, thrusting the photograph behind her. "I came with Tim." She read the look on his face. He was furious. "It wasn't my idea. Your mother insisted."

"How'd you get here?"

"Penny. And before you ask, I managed just fine." She edged toward the piano. "I'm a quick learner."

"Not so quick. Or you wouldn't be here with Tim. I suppose he's convinced you ride like Annie Oakley."

"Naturally." Charlotte groped her way to the piano, returning the photograph to its former position before Matthew realized what she'd been doing. She eased her fingers away. The heavy picture crashed down on the piano.

Matthew pushed her out of the way and looked at the photograph. "Snooping?"

There was no point in denying the obvious. "She was very beautiful."

"Where's Tim?"

"He went to the barn looking for you." Matthew clearly didn't want to talk of his wife, but Charlotte couldn't contain her curiosity. "How long was she ill?"

"She was shot to death." The clipped words reverberated around the room.

"Shot! Oh, Matthew, how terrible." Charlotte picked up the photograph and carefully settled it in its former resting place. Questions whirled in her head. Voicing any of them would be inexcusably rude.

"Before you reach any idiotic conclusions, let me assure you I didn't shoot her," he said with clipped sarcasm. "It was a drive-by gang shooting, in California. Lara happened to be standing on the wrong street corner at the wrong time."

"I didn't think you killed her," Charlotte gasped. "I know we have our differences, and you're arrogant, conceited and a major pain in the neck, but I'd never believe you were a murderer." She waved in the direction of the photographs. "It's obvious you loved your wife very much."

He gave her a long look, as if weighing up whether or not to believe her. Finally the muscles in his jaw eased. "Considering all the cause you've given me, I suppose the fact I haven't murdered you yet speaks well for my character."

"Now, Matthew," she chided him. "Let's not forget the little discussion we had earlier."

"I'm not likely to, cream puff."

"I believe calling me cream puff was one of the things I objected to."

"I believe it was. I also believe I said I'd give you my answer this evening. In the meantime—" he moved forward a couple of steps, penning Charlotte against the piano, his hands resting on the instrument on either side of her "—crossing into dangerous territory before any treaties are signed might have been pretty foolish, don't you think, cream puff?''

The edge of the piano lid bit into her spine. "You can't scare me, Matthew.''

"Can't I?'' he challenged softly

"No. I may not look tough, but I am. You, on the other hand, only look tough.''

"Don't kid yourself, cream puff. I'm tough all the way through.''

Tough he might be; overconfident and arrogant he definitely was. He was also standing much too close to her. "It's easier to chop down the biggest evergreen tree than to eradicate the smallest dandelion." If her knees were knocking, she had no intention of letting him know it.

"It's a funny thing—" he moved his hands to loosely grip her shoulders "—but I've always had a hankering to try dandelion wine.''

The heat of his hands flowed easily through the thin sleeves of her lacy blouse. A faint sunbeam caressed his weathered cheeks and accentuated the faint patch of stubble showing bluish against his tanned skin. His eyes were half-closed, long, dark lashes concealing his thoughts. He looked rough, tough and dangerously masculine. The kind of man she most disliked, Charlotte reminded herself. Hard-edged, iron-willed and absolutely devoted to having his own way, even if it meant trampling over everyone in his path. "Matthew, your attempts to bully me are ridiculous and won't work.''

"What's ridiculous is this hat. I don't think the sun is what you need protection from right now.'' He fumbled with the pins, and her straw hat sailed across the room.

Charlotte spared less than half a second worrying about the fate of the wooden cherries trimming the hat.

"I suppose that's your less-than-subtle way of saying I need protection from you." She ignored the hair tumbling down her back. "I won't be intimidated into signing the water rights over to you, Matthew, so you may as well save your energy for baby-sitting your cows."

He raised an eyebrow. "How could I possibly think I could intimidate a woman who likes to live as dangerously as you? This isn't about water or cows. It's about you, cream puff, and the mixed signals you send. Talking tough and looking soft. Wearing frilly feminine dresses and thin lacy blouses—" he brushed his knuckles down the buttoned front placket of her blouse "—that show nothing and promise everything. No coarse, androgynous jeans for you—" he lightly outlined her body with his hands "—just fancy trousers that draw a man's eye to your cute little bottom, or hip-swaying skirts that scent the air with tantalizing messages."

Charlotte swallowed hard. The kind of man who attracted her was gentle and kind and thoughtful. A man as different from Matthew as the Rocky Mountains differed from the Eastern plains. Blue eyes had always been her favorite. Eyes the color of flax or larkspur. Not eyes the color of mud. Only mud was a one-dimensional brown. Matthew's eyes were golden brown with fascinating brown flecks. Eyes that mocked her silence as he slowly pulled her against his body. Let him kiss her. His kisses meant nothing. It was mere chance his mouth had already learned how to please her.

Eventually Matthew lifted his head. "I think, cream puff," he drawled, his fingers weaving slowly through her hair, his thumbs drawing lazy circles beneath her ears, "you'd better run on back to Charlie's place before I decide you don't present the slightest impediment to my getting anything—" his eyes glinted wickedly at her "—I want."

*   *   *

Hours later Charlotte was still fuming. She wasn't sure if she was angrier at Matthew and his sarcastic amusement or at herself for retreating from the battle-field with all the haste and grace of a young pup running from his first encounter with a skunk. "Calling Matthew Thorneton a skunk is an insult to the animal. Don't you agree?" The rat in her lap opened one eye, stretched languorously and then curled back into a ball.

The smile on Charlotte's face disappeared as she caught sight of herself in the mirror. The cream-colored cotton sweater hugged her curves more closely than she'd remembered. Darn Matthew Thorneton. She was not going to permit his salacious comments to influence how she dressed. The way he talked a person would think she ran around half-naked. Lifting Snowball to her shoulder, Charlotte hiked up her long skirt of faded aqua-flowered sateen and reached for her nail polish. Riding boots took a terrible toll on painted toenails, and she had every intention of wearing her highest, flimsiest sandals this evening. Yes, and she'd sway her hips so widely she'd barely make it through any doorways. With luck she'd swing her hips so high, she'd bop Matthew Thorneton right between those diabolical brown eyes of his.

OK, those sexy brown eyes. Wiggling one set of wet toes, Charlotte propped up her other foot and dipped the small brush into the bright coral polish. She admitted it. On some juvenile level Matthew sent shimmers and tingles down her spine. On the other hand, so did exquisite old lace-trimmed linens and her grandmother's fudge, but she didn't lose her head over them. She dabbed paint on her last toenail. Nor was she going to lose her head over Matthew Thorneton.

"Hard at work, I see."

The brush jerked across her toe, leaving a trail of coral on her skin. Tim had run downstairs leaving her bedroom door open. "Now see what you made me do." Grabbing a tissue, she dabbed at the smear and concentrated on finishing the nail. Matthew's silent presence made her nervous, and she fumbled with the cap to the polish, barely averting disaster as the bottle threatened to tip from the dressing table. Lowering her skirt, she flapped the fabric above her toes to hasten the drying process.

"You made it safely back," Matthew said.

"Naturally." If he wanted to pretend their last conversation had never taken place, it was fine with her. "Penny delivered me here, just like taking a taxi."

"After your ride, did you give her a bath?" He filled the doorway, a folded towel in his hands.

Charlotte stood up and walked across the room. Hanging onto the bedpost, her back to him, she slipped her shoes on. "One of the employees was in the barn when we got back, and he and Tim showed me how to rub Penny down. You should have told me it wasn't called giving her a bath," she said with an injured air.

"If you didn't give Penny a bath, what do you suppose happened to all the hot water?"

Charlotte knew very well what had happened. Just before he'd come in, she'd drained the hot water tank. A cold shower was just what Matthew needed. She gave him a limpid glance over her shoulder. "I guess I used it all. I'm sorry." He didn't appear impressed with her apology. "You were wrong about riding Penny faster to work out the kinks in my muscles. If anything, my muscles were sorer today than yesterday. Soaking in the tub was definitely necessary. The water kept getting cold so I kept warming it up. I had no idea I'd used so much. After my bath I rinsed out a few—" she paused delicately "—unmentionables." Which she'd deliberately left hanging on the shower rod. Men were supposed to find dripping lingerie very irritating.

"Then these must be yours." Matthew shook out the towel and held up a pair of bikini panties and a brassiere. Hooking the brassiere on his finger, he swung it gently to and fro. "Somehow I suspected they might be. I couldn't quite see Mom in orange lace." Holding the bit of fabric up higher, he inspected it carefully. "No matter how little of it there is."

Charlotte set a new speed record crossing the room. She held out her hand. "The color is peach and I'll take those."

Matthew moved the garments just out of her reach. "Finders, keep—" He broke off.

"What's the matter?"

He was staring quizzically at her chest. "You appear to have three lumps as opposed to the usual feminine two."

"Oh, that." Brilliant conversation designed to distract him. At least she managed to retrieve her underwear.

"The lump in the middle is moving." His questioning gaze rose to her face.

The tiny claws running up her skin served notice it was too late to lie. "I'm, uh, baby-sitting." Snowball peered over the picot edging of her sweater neckline.

"Baby-sitting." Matthew's eyes narrowed. "With a rat?"

"He's kind of growing on me," Charlotte said airily. The small animal climbed out from her sweater, crawled under her loose-hanging hair and curled into a ball.

Matthew reached for Snowball's low-hanging tail and slid it through his fingers. "If you want to play games with me, cream puff, fine." The back of his hand grazed Charlotte's chest. "Just leave my son out of them."

"What's Tim got to do—?" The answer stopped her cold. Tossing her lingerie on the bed, she moved to sit at the dressing table. When she could trust herself to speak she said, "I know you dislike me. That's OK, because I don't like you much, either. But I wouldn't accuse you of deliberately harming a child anymore than I'd accuse you of murdering your wife." Her hand shook as she picked up an earring. "Just because you were prepared to cheat me on the matter of those water rights doesn't mean I'd use Tim to get back at you."

"If I'm wrong, I apologize."

"If? You don't believe me?"

"All I know is, one minute I see you quaking in your boots at the very thought of that rat, and the next minute, Snowball is free-ranging over your body."

"You saw what you wanted to see." She inserted a large gold hoop in one earlobe. "You were so busy hoping I'd barricade myself in my room, thoroughly terrorized by Snowball and your tales of him jumping from clocks and climbing into beds, it never occurred to you a girl—" she scornfully underlined the word "—might like rats. As it happens, I had a pet rat when I was younger." Nudging Snowball out of her way, she inserted the other earring. "I think white rats are cute and cuddly."

"Next you'll tell me snakes are adorable," Matthew said dryly.

Charlotte didn't have to fake a shudder. "Snakes. Ugh." Matthew was eyeing her oddly. She hoped she hadn't lost too much ground. It would never do to have Matthew suspect she was enacting a charade. Not when a significant part of her extremely brilliant plan to teach him a lesson depended on Matthew believing her the greenest of all greenhorns. She intended to out-dude every dude who ever confused a horse with a cow. What her plan, or Matthew's arrogance for that matter, had to do with her ultimate decision about the ranch she refused to delve too deeply into. Meanwhile, she set about repairing any damage. "I admit I wasn't too excited about rats at first. Grandad believed every child should have a pet to learn responsibility, but Aunt Faye is allergic to cats." No need for Matthew to know she'd rescued the rat from another child who, tiring of his pet, intended to gas it. Charlotte embroidered her tale. "Dogs jump on you and get your clothes dirty, and I couldn't abide cleaning goldfish bowls." She shivered dramatically, her earrings banging against the sides of her neck. "I considered a hamster, but a friend had one and it bit. Birds are so messy." She shuddered again for emphasis. "So I got a rat." Her earlobe was violently tugged. "Ouch!"

"What's the matter?"

"Snowball is caught in my earring." Capturing the rat's head, she tried to push him back through the large gold hoop. The harder she pushed, the more the animal resisted. He shook his head, his every movement causing the earring wire to tug painfully on her earlobe. "Quit fighting me, you pestilent rodent."

"Stand up and let me get him." Moving to her side, Matthew brushed her hair behind her ear and took hold of Snowball. "Hold still, both of you."

"What are you guys doing?"

"Your father is torturing me." Charlotte winced as the rat squealed. "And enjoying it entirely too much."

Matthew laughed. "Your little friend has gotten himself into a most ridiculous predicament."

"Gosh," Tim said. "How'd he do that? Careful, Dad. Don't hurt him."

"Sure. Rip my ear off, but don't hurt Snowball."

"Pay no attention to her, Tim. A little bit of pain and women go crazy. There." Matthew handed the liberated animal to his son. "That should teach him to keep his nose out of other people's earrings."

"I wouldn't count on it," Charlotte said, stroking the rat's back with her finger. "Is he all right?"

"He'll live. Go put him up, Tim, so he can recover from his trauma."

"His trauma," Charlotte echoed indignantly as Tim left the room. "What about my trauma? Not to mention my ear."

"Let me see." Matthew pushed her head to one side and ran his fingers over her lobe. "I don't see any damage. You'll both survive." His fingers gently massaged her tingling earlobe.

Charlotte made the mistake of turning her head. Matthew's face was only inches from hers. Brown eyes warm with amusement met her gaze, and then his eyes darkened with a message as ancient as Adam and Eve. And as easy to read as a kindergarten primer. A sudden breeze came through the open bedroom window, riffling the hem of her skirt and bringing the scent of pine. There was a flash of lightning, and thunder boomed in the distance, but the heavy tension in the room had nothing to do with the outside elements. Charlotte forgot how to breathe.

"I think the time has come," Matthew said coolly, "to discuss your proposal."

CHAPTER SEVEN

NERVOUS adrenaline surged through Charlotte's body. Though why she should be nervous...she had everything to gain and nothing to lose. Sitting down, she picked up a comb and ran it through her hair. "What's to discuss?" Her voice sounded almost as cool as Matthew's. "All I require from you is yes or no."

"Maybe that's not all I require from you." Matthew stood looking at her, his shoulders braced against the wall.

Charlotte braided her hair down the back of her head. "Matthew, let us not forget here, I'm the one who has the water rights and you're the one who wants them."

"I have to tell you, cream puff, excuse me, Charlotte," he said with excessive politeness, "I'm getting a little tired of that sword being held over my head."

Tying a ribbon at the end of her braid, Charlotte held Matthew's gaze in the mirror. "I'm not."

Matthew laughed wryly. "At least you're honest—" he crossed booted feet and tucked his thumbs in jeans pockets "—even if your proposal is juvenile, ludicrously stupid and totally unworkable."

"Gosh, Matthew, you don't have to sugarcoat your opinion for me," Charlotte mocked.

"I can go along with the notion of a truce—"

"How magnanimous."

"But the rest of it..." He shook his head. "Won't work, cream puff."

She raised her eyebrows at his image in the mirror.

"Excuse me. Charlotte."

"Why not?"

"You can't seriously expect me to work with you trailing along behind me for the rest of your stay. You have no clue what's involved in running an operation like mine."

"Surely it's in your best interest to show me. Otherwise I might decide to keep Mr. Gannen's place. As sort of a weekend hobby or vacation cabin."

Matthew snorted. "A ranch isn't a hobby. You'd run the place into the ground before you knew what hit you."

"If I go bankrupt, I can always sell those water rights to the highest bidder, can't I?"

"Damn it, Charlotte, you don't even own a pair of jeans. Charlie never said you had to turn into a rancher. Why can't you be sensible? Sit on the porch swing, sip some lemonade and enjoy your vacation. If you want to ride Penny I'll arrange for one of the hands to go out with you for a couple of hours a day."

"I don't want to ride with one of the hands."

"Why not?" His eyes narrowed. "Afraid if you try to grind some honest cowboy under your heel he'll up and throw his job in your face?"

Charlotte ran her thumb over the teeth of the comb. "Of course," she cordially agreed. "The great Matthew Thorneton, on the other hand, has a great deal more at stake. Doesn't he?"

"The great Matthew Thorneton doesn't like having a gun held to his head," he said tightly.

Charlotte squeezed her hand, the comb's teeth biting deeply into her palm. "Neither do I, Matthew. I wanted nothing to do with Charles Gannen, his ranch or his wishes. I didn't want to come here, and I don't want to be here. Yet here I am."

"That's not my fault. I didn't write the will. I only delivered the message."

"No, Matthew, you did more than that. You played my mother, my aunt and my grandmother as if they were violins and you a virtuoso violinist. If you'd accepted my refusal when I gave it to you at the store, I wouldn't be here now. So all this is definitely your fault. I'm getting nothing out of—"

"The money you'll get for selling the ranch to me."

"There isn't enough money to pay me for having to endure being here. No, Matthew, as I see it, all the rewards go to you. You get the water and you get to give the ranch to your mother. I think the stakes here are much higher for you than for me." His face gave her no clue to his thoughts as he watched her in the mirror.

"I see," he said slowly. "You don't want to be here and have decided it's my fault you are. We're actually talking about some childish, perverted notion of revenge. You want to disrupt my entire life, stick your nose where it doesn't belong and generally be a pain in the—" he barely paused "—neck. In return you'll sell to me something you don't want and have no use for."

She gave him a sincere look. "I said I'll sell you Charles Gannen's ranch, including the water rights and everything else, at a fair price agreed upon by both. All I'm asking in exchange is that you allow me to familiarize myself with ranch life by accompanying you as you go about your business."

"Why?"

"For my mother. She knows nothing of ranch living and her time with Chick Gannen was so short. If I can tell her and show her photographs of what ranch life is really like, her image of him will be more complete." At Matthew's skeptical face, she decided there was nothing to lose by telling the truth. She peered at him from beneath lowered lashes, a faint smile playing at the corners of her mouth. "Why should I be the only one inconvenienced?"

"This is rough country, Charlotte. A soft tenderfoot could get hurt."

"I have confidence in your ability to keep me out of trouble." Surprisingly, she did.

He raised his eyebrows at that before saying, "When I give you orders, Charlotte, I'd expect you to obey them. Instantly."

"If they're reasonable."

"I don't give unreasonable orders," Matthew said coolly. "I also want your promise you won't cry and whine and complain from dawn to dusk. I want your promise you won't run back to Denver the first time you break a fingernail or get a smudge of dirt on your clothes."

"Do you want my promise in writing? We can go into Durango and get it notarized."

"Forget notarizing anything. Your promise in writing, and we send a copy to your aunt. Miss Darnelle strikes me as the kind who's death on promise breakers."

Charlotte made a face at his accurate reading. Standing up, she held out her hand. "Do we have a deal then, Matthew?"

He stared at her hand for a long moment before folding his own large one around it. "If I had a horse this stupid, I'd get rid of him." Releasing her hand, he turned and left.

"Matthew," Charlotte called after him. "Don't forget our truce. You're supposed to be nice to me, too."

Matthew stuck his head around the door. "I'm a human being, cream puff, not a damned saint."

Which told her exactly what she was getting herself into. She questioned whether exacting revenge against

Matthew would be worth the price he'd undoubtedly attempt to make her pay. Despite her threats, she knew the smart and easy way of wiping Charles Gannen and his intrusive will out of her life would be to sell everything to Matthew. The money wouldn't come amiss. She and Aunt Faye were the only wage earners in the family, and Aunt Faye was getting on in years. The store was only profitable because the two of them paid themselves low wages.

It wasn't as if she were considering keeping the ranch. She didn't want the ranch. She didn't want to live on the ranch. Ranching wasn't in her blood; all her genes came from her mother. Playing cowgirl for two weeks was ridiculously stupid. One would think she'd fallen off Penny and landed on her head. The whole idea was as dumb as her begging her mother to send her to a riding camp all those summers when she was growing up. Not that she'd had to beg very hard. Her mother had fallen in with Charlotte's wishes so quickly Charlotte had been astonished. Only later had she realized her mother naively expected Charles Gannen to relent and invite Charlotte to his ranch.

Charlotte smoothed down a stray hair. Stupidity must run in the Darnelle family. If she knew anything about men like Matthew Thorneton, he was going to do his level best to make the remainder of her stay an absolute living hell. The trick was in making it more miserable for him. Absentmindedly she rubbed her tender earlobe, wondering what kind of devilment Matthew would devise in an effort to send her scurrying back to the security of the porch swing. As long as he continued to believe she was the rawest, wimpiest tenderfoot, Charlotte was positive she could handle anything he dreamed up. She was wrong.

"What do you mean, Tim's gone?"

Matthew helped himself to more pancakes. "He's spending the rest of your visit with Lara's parents."

"You sent him away?" Charlotte asked in a choked voice. Now she understood why Matthew had allowed her to sleep late this morning when she'd been expecting a predawn wake-up call. He'd needed time to sneak away his son.

Helen handed Charlotte a glass of juice. "I still don't understand why you took Tim over there now. He was having such a good time with Charlotte being here."

"My being here is exactly why Tim was banished," Charlotte said tightly.

"You have him all year," Matthew said to his mother. "It's not so strange his other grandparents want him for awhile. You know they'd like him and Paula to be closer, and they never can count on her being home long."

"That one," Helen said in disgust. "It was probably her idea. She wants Tim at her folks' place because she can't figure out how else to get you over there."

"She doesn't even call him by name. 'Your son' is how she refers to him." Two hours later as the pickup bounced down a ranch road, Charlotte was still hurt and furious. "And if she harms Snowball, I'll never forgive you."

"Actually, I promised Tim you'd take care of Snowball while he's gone." He slanted a look at her. "For some reason Tim trusts you to keep Snowball healthy and happy."

"It's nice to know one of the Thorneton males thinks I can be trusted. Or is it less a matter of not trusting me around Tim and more a matter of sending him away because you're mad at me?"

"What one has to do with the other is beyond me."

"It's not beyond me. Sending him away was your way of saying I'm such a despicable person I'd deliberately harm Tim in order to score off you. I know you don't like me, but I can't believe you think I'm that cruel." Charlotte angrily wiped moisture from her cheek. "I hate you, but Tim's my friend and you know it." She sniffed. "You made me promise not to cry or the agreement is off, but if you thought your acting so ugly would force me into crying, you're wrong, because I'm not crying, so don't think you can weasel out of our agreement." Only the seat belt kept her from flying through the windshield as Matthew braked to an abrupt halt.

"Damn it, Charlotte," he yelled, facing her. "Quit acting like you're in a TV soap opera. I wasn't thinking of you at all when I decided to take Tim to the Kenton place. I was thinking of Tim. He's my son and I have to protect him the way I think best. No—" he forestalled her angry comment "—I don't mean protect him from you. At least, not in the way you think. I apologize if taking Tim to the Kentons hurt your feelings. That was never my intent." He turned away, staring straight ahead. "But even knowing it would hurt you, I'd do it again." After a second he went on. "Last year in school, Tim's class made Mother's Day presents. Some smart-mouthed kid told Tim he couldn't make one since he didn't have a mother." His voice was bleak. "Mom does her best, but I know I ought to marry and give Tim a mother." Matthew rubbed the outer rim of the steering wheel with the palm of one hand. "When it comes right down to it, however, I've never been able to. Marriage means more to me than a convenience."

Charlotte immediately thought of the day years ago when she'd taken Grandpa Darnelle to school on a Bring Your Dad Day. Remarks made by some of the other children had cut deep. "While I can appreciate your concern, I think you're overreacting. Tim and I are just friends.''

"Don't kid yourself. Last night when Tim was getting ready for bed, he asked me if I thought you were pretty. When I said yes, he told me one of his friends had a new baby sister. Then he said he wouldn't mind a baby sister.'' Matthew gave her a level look. "A baby sister with red curly hair.''

His words startled a nervous giggle from Charlotte. "Whatever else Tim is,'' she said in response to Matthew's raised eyebrows, "he's definitely not very good at reading people. The thought of you and me...''

"Which is why Tim is at the Kentons. There's no point in him getting his hopes up or building air castles. If he saw us spending day after day together, he'd imagine something quite different from reality.''

"All you'd have to do is explain to him that—''

"His good friend Charlotte is blackmailing me?''

"Why not?'' Charlotte asked slowly. "That would surely convince him I'm hardly mother or wife material.''

"What would Tim care about a spot of blackmail when he's found him a woman who likes rats?'' Matthew started the truck.

A mourning dove sounded plaintively through the open truck window. A mixture of sadness and pity settled over Charlotte. Sadness at the unfairness of life. Pity for Matthew, for Tim. And for a child who'd never had a father to read to her, to hear her evening prayers, to hold her on his lap, to banish her nightmares. Charlotte struggled to rein in her thoughts. She'd managed just fine with only one parent. It was Tim who thought he needed a full set. Tim who needed a mother.

"If you're applying, let me remind you Tim's mother would be my wife.''

She hadn't realized she'd spoken aloud, but at least sparring with Matthew distracted her from profitless thoughts. "As if I'd want to marry you. The minute I saw you I knew you were a man who'd put his wife in a flannel nightgown."

"There's nothing wrong with flannel."

"Matthew," Charlotte said, injecting her voice with the proper horror, "tell me you never, ever bought your wife a flannel nightgown."

Matthew pulled over to the side of the road and parked. "Lara liked it," he said coldly.

Charlotte threw up her hands. "That settles it. Tell Tim no red-haired baby sisters. Not with a dad who buys flannel nightgowns for his wife." She flinched as the driver's door slammed shut. Who'd want red-haired babies anyway? Towheaded babies were sweeter. With brown eyes. She frowned. There were no brown eyes in the Darnelle family. Which was just as well. Brown-eyed babies undoubtedly were demanding, obstreperous and difficult to get along with. Just look how they grew up. She grabbed her camera and scrambled out of the pickup.

Matthew stood in back of the truck, his hands clenching the top of the tailgate. "Just for the record, my wife did not leave me because I bought her a damned flannel nightgown."

For a second, Charlotte could only gape in confusion at him. A confusion quickly replaced by chagrin as she belatedly realized she'd trespassed on private territory and stumbled across a mine field. "Matthew, I didn't mean...I never intended...I was just babbling. Whatever happened between you and your wife...please—" She touched his arm as the tailgate dropped with a loud clang. "I'm sorry if I inadvertently caused you pain."

Drawing on a pair of worn leather gloves, he rolled a spool of wire toward him. "You don't have the power to cause me pain."

So much for apologies to arrogant cowboys. A second's reflection blunted most of Charlotte's indignation. Matthew had undoubtedly been thinking of his wife and the pain he still felt over her death. Remembering Paula's claim that Lara had left Matthew, Charlotte wondered if that eased or deepened his grief. And she wondered why Matthew's first wife had left him. She knew better than to ask. The silence had stretched too long. Charlotte sought a safe topic. "A rat is an unusual pet for a kid living on a ranch."

Matthew almost smiled. "I thought Charlie was going to have a coronary when Tim hauled Snowball home. Ranchers don't exactly cotton to rodents." He clipped a length of wire and headed toward the sagging fence alongside the road.

"You let Tim keep Snowball even though Charles Gannen disapproved?"

"You have to quit thinking Charlie and I were clones. We disagreed on a number of issues." Matthew wired a loose strand of fence to the post. "Tim's dog had died of cancer a couple of months before. He was pretty cut up about it. Considering everything—" he twisted the pliers with a vicious movement, a small spasm rippling through his jaw muscles "—letting him keep the rat seemed the least I could do for him."

"What if Mr. Gannen had refused to allow the rat in his house?"

"Bring me the fence stretcher out of the back." At her blank look, he described the tool. When she'd handed it to him, he hooked the stretcher to a wire and began tightening it. "I guess Tim and I would have moved back to my place. It would have made things tougher, but we'd have managed."

"You'd have defied Mr. Gannen for Tim?"

"Sure." He yanked on the strand of wire. "I'm his father." He hooked the stretcher onto the next strand. "If Chick had lived, he'd have taken on the world for your sake."

Charlotte lowered the camera. "I'm past the age of fairy tales, Matthew. Chick Gannen would have dumped me as easily as he dumped my mother."

Matthew straightened up, looking at her in surprise. "He was killed in Vietnam. You blame him for that? You think he wanted to die? What kind of screwy thinking is that?"

"No, I don't think he wanted to die," Charlotte said shortly. "But I don't think he planned to come home to my mom, either. Grandpa Darnelle told me Charles Gannen was honestly stunned when my mother called. Chick had never written a word about her."

"And you decided he was never serious about your mom."

She shrugged. "It doesn't take a brain surgeon. He was going away to war and wanted to make a little whoopee with a pretty girl before he left."

"Chick wasn't like that." Matthew replaced the tools in the bed of the pickup and climbed behind the steering wheel. His eyes fixed on the horizon, he made no move to turn on the ignition. After a long moment, he said, "Fasten your seat belt." Her obedience taken for granted, the pickup took off with a roar, a wide plume of dust in its wake.

"You just passed some downed fence," Charlotte shouted. "Isn't this your land?" A particularly deep rut smashed her teeth together; they barely missed chomping down on her tongue. She decided, under the circumstances, even her mother wouldn't expect her to make polite conversation. By the time Matthew brought the pickup to a skidding halt, he'd zigged and zagged, traveling down one unfamiliar, dusty road after another, until she had no clue where they were.

Matthew waved his hand down the road before them. "This is Gannen land on your right. The other side of the road, that used to be Maywell land. Connie sold it to some guy from Denver after her folks died. By then, Charlie didn't care, but twenty-five years ago, all he could think about was how Maywell land would become Gannen land once Chick and Connie got hitched."

"Are you trying to tell me Chick hadn't gotten around to mentioning Mom to his father because of some stupid land?"

"Land is never stupid to a rancher. Chick knew what his marrying Connie meant to Charlie, and he wouldn't have taken his dad's dreams lightly. He knew exactly what he was giving up for love. Proving he loved your mother very much. Proving he would have returned for her."

"You haven't proven anything. In fact, one could conclude exactly the opposite," Charlotte said slowly. "If this land meant so much to Charles Gannen, and by extension, his son, then all the more reason to believe Chick would never have married my mother instead of Connie."

Matthew gave her a penetrating look. "I think I've been missing something here. It was clear you had no love lost for Charlie, but I never realized you hate your father, too."

"Don't be silly." The pickup cab was too confining. She jumped out and walked over to the fenced field. Matthew followed her. "I don't have any feelings about him at all." A scraggly wild rose fought for existence beside an old log fence post, the plant's blossoms bright pink against the gray, weathered wood.

Matthew snapped off one of the blossoms and handed it to Charlotte. "I was out riding one day and saw Chick digging. I rode over to see what he was doing. He'd been checking fence, a pasture where they were getting ready to move some cows in. Chick was digging up some kind of flower. I could see it wasn't locoweed or anything poisonous to cows, so I asked him why he was digging it up. I can still see him, standing there, one foot on the shovel, his hat shoved back, while he explained he was taking it, a wild rose, to his mom for near the house because, 'Cows don't appreciate beauty, Matt,' he said. Most cowboys would have passed the rose without thought, or at the most considered it a shame the cows would trample it, but not Chick. He took the time and trouble to move it."

"I don't see the point of—"

"Chick had two dogs. One he picked up along the road after a car hit it. Never did find the owner. Charlie thought they ought to shoot the poor thing, put him out of his misery, but Chick drove him in to the vet's. That dog turned out to be the best darned cattle-herding dog. Chick named him Trey because he got along better on three legs than most dogs do on four. Hunter showed up during duck-hunting season. He was a bird dog, been shot in the head, blinded in one eye. No one claimed him, either. There were other dogs, earlier dogs, before my time. My dad said hurt critters just naturally found Chick."

"So he was a paragon." Rose petals dotted the ground at her feet. "Big deal. If you think babbling a bunch of maudlin nonsense is going to make me put Chick Gannen up on some marble pedestal, you're wrong. I don't care if he kicked dogs or rose them from the dead."

"No," Matthew said mildly, "but your mom might."

"She already worships the ground he walks on." A bee buzzed loudly in the stark silence. "I didn't mean that the way it sounded," Charlotte said at last.

"Your mom must have suffered a great deal when Chick was killed. Never marrying, raising a child by herself...your mom's had a difficult time. Resenting the man who left her in that situation is understandable."

"She doesn't resent him."

"No, I don't suppose she ever did."

Charlotte played with a barb projecting from a strand of wire, repeatedly snagging the tip of her glove and pulling it away. "All right, yes, I do resent him. Not on my account, but on Mom's." His silence goaded her into further speech. "OK, maybe I did hate him for abandoning us, but that's when I was little. It doesn't matter any more. Growing up as I did forced me to be independent and tough."

"Yup." Matthew flicked one of the huge silk peach-colored roses adorning her hat. "The first time I saw you, I thought to myself, 'Now there's one tough cookie.' It must have been the ruffles that made me think so."

"For your information, Matthew Thorneton, arrogant, egotistical cowboys don't have a monopoly on toughness." Charlotte snapped a photograph of the rose-decorated fence and flounced to the pickup. "Furthermore," she added loftily, "real men don't judge their women on how much weight they can bench press. Not everyone's definition of tough is the ability to push around a bunch of cows, ride a bucking bronco, chew tobacco and skin a buffalo."

Matthew shook his head, his eyes gleaming with suppressed laughter. "I sure would have loved to have seen you and Charlie go head to head. He'd have gotten you so riled the sparks would have flown from that red hair

of yours. Yup,'' he drawled, ''I figure Charlie's dying
before you got here deprived his friends of a downright
entertaining war.''

"My hair is not red,'' Charlotte said coldly. "And
entertaining the locals was never my goal.''

Nor had her goal been to entertain Matthew. Infuriate
him, yes. Entertain him, no. Unfortunately, Matthew,
through some ill-deserved twist of dumb luck, had hit
upon the one response to Charlotte's plan that rendered
the plan a total waste of time and energy. Matthew was
entertained. And amused. And even worse, unfor-
givably worse, he was patient. She'd begged to assist him,
then handed him the wrong tools. She'd dropped a
wrench on his toe and spilled fence paint down his back.
She'd tripped him, belted him across the rear with a fence
board and tumbled against him twice when dismounting
Penny. She thought she'd glimpsed a slight tightening of
his jaw a couple of times, especially the time she'd shoved
him into a cow pie, but to her surprise, he'd yet to raise
his voice, much less look as if he was seriously considering slugging her. He accepted her breathless
apologies and artless explanations as if he truly believed
he was a victim of Charlotte's overeagerness and
inexperience.

Lying in bed at night, Charlotte reluctantly faced the
truth that if Matthew weren't quite so patient, she
wouldn't be escalating her efforts to antagonize him. Not
that she wanted him to slug her. She merely wanted to
get under his skin. There was no point in falling off her
horse and practically knocking Matthew down if he was
going to say stupid things such as she shouldn't be dis-
heartened because he was sure he could see improvement. If Matthew saw any improvement in her
riding skills then he was blinder than that stupid dog of
Chick Gannen's. Sometimes Charlotte almost suspected

that Matthew, well aware she was deliberately engineering all the "accidents", was toying with her for purposes of his own.

The man who'd been demanding and abrupt in her store had proven to be patient on his home ground. Charlotte supposed nature was a harsh instructor in the art of patience. Cows and horses gave birth when they wanted, and rain fell when the heavenly conditions were right. Winter blew in when it was ready and gave way to spring only when it was so inclined. Ranchers, she'd learned, of necessity lived according to the rhythm of their land.

Ranchers, also of necessity, were jacks-of-all-trades. Matthew was as comfortable on a tractor as he was on a horse. And although she doubted the boss routinely fixed fence or changed oil in the ranch vehicles or checked for stray calves, his expertise demonstrated he'd done at one time or another every chore on the ranch. Matthew was part mechanic, part electrician, part veterinarian and part bookkeeper.

And all cowboy, she reminded herself, eyeing his back as he slouched in the saddle on Jay's back. The gelding's long stride drew him away from Penny. Charlotte slowed the mare even more, widening the distance between the two horses. The trail rose over a small hill and turned. Matthew and his horse disappeared from sight. "Matthew!" she cried. "Where are you? Matthew! Matthew!" Reining Penny in a circle, Charlotte silently blessed the agreeable mare.

Matthew appeared over the horizon, coming at an easy canter. "What's the matter?"

"I thought I was lost. I looked around and you weren't anywhere in sight. How could you go off and leave me?"

"Don't worry, cream puff. I won't let you get lost. Where we're going is right over the hill."

"Oh, look at the babies," Charlotte crooned as they crested the hill. "Can I pet them?"

"If you'll recall, the last time you wanted to pet some calves, one cow looked at you and you ran screaming at me, knocking me flat."

"It's not my fault you keep vicious animals. She did more than look—she charged me." Charlotte could swear Matthew came close to sighing.

"She was walking toward you because she was curious. She'd probably never seen orange flowers on a hat." He leaned down to open the gate. "Just stay on Penny, keep her to a walk and try to keep out of trouble."

"What exactly are we doing here?"

"Well, cream puff, I'm checking stock. What you're doing here—" he fastened the gate behind her "—I'm not real sure."

Most of the time Charlotte was no longer sure, either. It was almost as if she and Matthew were engaged in some kind of battle, and leaving him to go peacefully about his work would be the same as conceding he'd won. The distasteful notion stiffened her resolve. This time, for once, when a cowboy went up against a lady, the lady was definitely going to win. Even if she had to abandon a few ladylike ideas such as truth and fair play.

CHAPTER EIGHT

THE small pond shimmered in the midday sun. Wild iris flagged blue along the water, and white lilies and blue flax waved breezily from an adjoining pasture. Dark pines and light green aspen mingled on the sides of the distant mesa. Matthew fastened another gate behind them. "We'll eat lunch here."

"Here? Am I supposed to share my sandwich with every hungry cow that comes along?"

"Since they're beef sandwiches, I'd be leery of offering any to a cow," Matthew said deadpan. "The cow might take offense."

"I'll stay on Penny's back while I eat, thank you very much."

Matthew laughed, walking up to grab Penny's reins. "Get down, cream puff. We moved the cattle out of here several weeks ago." He watered the horses, then moved them to the shade of a nearby cottonwood tree. Returning with a pouch, he held out a small Thermos and a brown sack. "Chow time."

Hugging her lunch to her, Charlotte slowly pivoted. "You don't really expect me to sit on the ground, in the dirt?"

"Shucks, cream puff—" he sprawled in the shade of a large bush "—you're beyond any man's expectation."

The ambiguous statement didn't merit delving into. Looking around, she spotted a large, flat rock. Beside it lay a small leafy branch. Charlotte poked warily at the rock, checking for any unsavory creatures lurking in the vicinity, then she brushed the top with the leafy

132

branch. The area secure, she gripped her lunch sack with her teeth, set her gloves on a nearby bush and tugged a white lacy handkerchief from a breast pocket of her violet linen blouse. Dampening the dainty square with water from the Thermos, she scrubbed at her hands. Matthew was watching her. "Your neck scarf?" she mumbled around the sack.

Without a word he untied and handed her his bandanna.

Charlotte draped the navy blue print square over the rock and carefully sat down on it. She opened her lunch sack.

Matthew munched on a potato chip. "If you'd accept Mom's offer of a pair of her jeans, a little dirt wouldn't matter."

She looked down her nose at him. "I didn't come here to turn into a cowhand. I'm not going to cut my hair short, wear men's overalls, chew tobacco or learn to swear with your skill." She bit daintily into her sandwich, chewed in what she hoped was a refined manner and swallowed. "My mother raised a lady."

Matthew grinned. "Sometimes I have a sneaking suspicion your last statement would be news to her."

Her eyebrows shot up. "Your mother, nice and sweet as she is, certainly didn't raise a gentleman."

"She likes you, too." He disregarded the rest of her comment.

Charlotte crumbled a potato chip. "I thought she might resent me."

"Because of the will? She's always felt bad she couldn't persuade Charlie to recognize you. She knows the will was Charlie's way of telling her to mind her own business, but she thinks having you here is worth the price she's paying. I don't know how you managed to pull the wool over her eyes, cream puff. Maybe I should have packed her off to the Kenton place, too."

"Goodness, Matthew, to hear you talk one would think I'm a tornado, bubonic plague and the atom bomb all wrapped up in one."

"No," he said slowly, "you're more dangerous."

"Don't tell me I frighten—" she fluttered her lashes at him "—a big, bad cowboy like you."

"You scare the hell out of me," he said frankly.

She gazed skyward. "I shall treasure this moment forever. The arrogant Matthew Thorneton admitting to fear." She returned her gaze to his face and asked avidly, "What is it about me that frightens you, Matthew? You must tell me. I'm simply agog to learn how a mere insignificant female can, how did you so delicately put it, scare the hell out of you?"

"It's no joke, cream puff. You dropped into our lives with painted toes and fancy underwear and expensive perfumes. You smile and swish your ruffled skirts and show off your fancy city ways, and Mom and Tim are mesmerized, fooled into thinking they've become your friends, when the truth is, you're only using them to entertain yourself."

"That's not true," she said, aghast.

"Mom's so dazzled by you, she actually told me she thinks you're sensible. Sensible." He snorted. "You're playing gracious lady now, but as soon as your two weeks are up, you'll run right back to the city and forget you ever knew a poor motherless kid and a middle-aged widow. Did you ever stop to think how badly your behavior is going to hurt them?"

All urge to tease him fled. Charlotte looked at her sandwich. "I'm not like that."

"What are you like, cream puff? You've been here over a week, and I'll be damned if I have a clue as to what makes you tick. You wrap yourself in so many layers of gilt and fluff, it's hard to tell if there's a real person inside.''

Charlotte knew she should be congratulating herself for successfully hiding her inner self from Matthew. Except she didn't feel triumphant. Instead, she felt somehow empty. It was Matthew's fault, she argued internally. He was the one who'd dismissed her as all-sugar, no-substance cotton candy. He was the one who made her into a nonperson, a person who felt forced to invent herself for his benefit. She whipped up her anger against him, the anger a feeble substitute for the hurt he'd inflicted. He had no right to find fault with the person he'd forced her into portraying. Even if she were all gilt and fluff, which she wasn't, which he'd know if he'd ever cared to find out, even if she were, she'd never hurt Tim and Helen. He was blind and stupid and a dumb cowboy. He was also watching her curiously, as if he really expected her to answer his question. ''What am I like?'' she mused. ''My friends think I'm loyal. My grandmother thinks I'm kind. My mother thinks I'm special. My aunt thinks I'm clever.'' She gave him a false smile. ''Does that answer your question?''

''You omitted a few characteristics.''

''Such as silly? Or ridiculous? Or stupid? It may surprise you, Matthew, but most people don't think of me in those terms.''

He stretched out on his back, his folded arms pillowing his head. His voice came from beneath the hat shielding his face. ''I was thinking more along the lines of hot-tempered, illogical, irritating, contrary and just plain stubborn.''

Charlotte carefully brushed the crumbs from her lap and stood up, stuffing the debris from her lunch into the paper sack. ''You forgot prissy.''

"Ah, prissy. I'm beginning to like prissy. And red hair and freckles. I suspect it's possible I'll miss all three when you abandon us for the city."

Her wadded-up lunch sack scored a direct hit on his belt buckle. "I won't miss your egotistical arrogance," she snapped.

Matthew raised his hat. "Did I mention hot-tempered?"

One minute he was accusing her of unconscionable behavior; the next minute he was laughing at her. As if she were nothing. As if she were irritating, but basically harmless. She'd show him harmless. She'd show him irritating. And if he was so darned fond of hot-tempered, she'd show him hot-tempered.

Matthew gathered up the horses and led them to the pond. Handing Penny's reins to Charlotte, he stowed the lunch remains away, then stood at the water's edge, his back to Charlotte, waiting patiently for the horses to finish. Revengeful was a characteristic he'd missed, Charlotte thought. He should have remembered revengeful. She nudged Penny slightly to one side and screamed. Not a loud, piercing scream that curdled the blood and caused neck hairs to stand at attention. Not the kind of caterwauling scream that stampeded horses. But a little choking scream, just loud enough to startle Penny into turning to investigate. Naturally, as Penny's front section swung toward Charlotte, her hindquarters swung in the other direction, smack into Matthew's unsuspecting back. Matthew landed facedown in the lake. For a very brief second Charlotte thought the wild iris were doubled over in laughter. Matthew's splashing from the pond chased away whimsical thoughts. She schooled her face to show a mixture of sympathy and contrition and held out her hand. "I'm so sorry, Matthew. Are you OK?"

Wordlessly he stomped up to dry land, ignoring her outstretched hand. Sitting down, he yanked off his boots and poured the water from them. His shirt was next, methodically unbuttoned, removed and tightly wrung. Water streamed from the faded tan twill. He draped the shirt over a bush and without looking up said, "I assume you have an explanation. Not that I'll believe it."

"A snake, Matthew. A rattlesnake."

Giving her a sharp look, he jumped to his feet. "Where?" Ignoring that his feet were clad in nothing but wet socks, he strode across the pasture to where she'd been standing. "Come show me. Where did it go? How big was it?"

"Huge." Charlotte shuddered. "I'm not coming anywhere near there. It was at least eighteen inches and bright green."

"Green." Matthew gave her a disgusted look. "Rattlesnakes aren't green."

"I heard him rattle." She wished he'd put his shirt back on. Wrestling cows and horses around sculpted a man's body in disturbingly attractive ways. Tanned skin indicated he wasn't averse to working without his shirt.

"If you heard anything other than your overactive imagination, you heard the snake moving through dry leaves or grass." He picked a few burrs from his socks before wringing the water from the heavy fabric. "If there was a snake."

"Just because you're so clumsy and fell in the lake is no reason to call me a liar." Charlotte started toward Penny. An iron trap caught her leg above her boot. One tug and she was falling. She landed squarely in the middle of Matthew's lap. Steel bands prevented her from scrambling up. "Let go of me. What do you think you're doing?"

Matthew grinned. "Protecting you. From snakes."

She liked neither his grin nor the wide expanse of warm, muscled flesh so close to her face. "You're the only snake around here."

"Then you admit it? There was no snake, just an excuse to dunk me in the pond."

"I meant," she said stiffly, her eyes glued to his chin, "there is no other snake right here. The other snake—"

"The bright green rattlesnake."

"—was over there by the pond."

"Well," Matthew drawled, not loosening his grip one iota, "snakes move like greased lightning. One second over there, the next over here. Better to be safe than sorry."

"I'd rather be sorry."

"If you insist."

She should have known he'd retaliate. His chest had dried, and his skin radiated the warmth of the early afternoon sun. As did his mouth. His kisses were almost familiar territory now, but no less exciting for that. She shivered and nestled closer as his hand curved around the back of her neck. Her hands found their way up his arms until they clung to his silken, muscled shoulders. Her lips parted, welcoming his deepening the kiss. His hand tugged her blouse loose and slid inside, his work-roughened fingertips barely grazing her skin, igniting her nerve endings. He outlined the wisp of lace and silk circling her body. Charlotte's breasts grew heavy and warm. And confined. And then the imprisoning silk was gone and blessedly cool air kissed the tightening tips. Except now coolness wasn't what she wanted. Matthew's rugged callused palm, with knowing, tender moves, gave her what she sought. Charlotte melted into his touch. Leaning backward, Matthew tugged her to stretch out along his length.

"Damn!"

The explosive word Matthew uttered deep in her mouth brought Charlotte to her senses. She struggled to her feet as he released her. "I... You..." A passing breeze sent a chill through her lower extremities, directing her attention downward. Her riding jodhpurs were almost as wet as Matthew's jeans. "Look what you did," she cried, buttoning her blouse, endeavoring to blot from her mind the activity she'd so recently engaged in. "I'll probably catch pneumonia." She didn't care why he'd sworn. She knew why he'd broken off the kiss. She wasn't Lara.

"You weren't worried I'd get pneumonia," he said wryly.

Charlotte tucked her blouse carefully into her trousers, then fussed with the collar, needlessly straightening it. His not saying anything about their kiss finally propelled her into speech. "I suppose cowboys make love to women in pastures so they'll have something to brag about to the other boys at the bar." She retrieved her hat from the ground. When had it come off?

Matthew pulled boots on over wet socks. "Is that why ladies—" he subtly underlined the word "—roll around in pastures? So they can trot home to their city friends and make fun of the poor dumb cowboys who fell for their perfumed airs and graces?" He brushed off his back and yanked on his shirt, shoving the ends in his jeans.

"I suppose you're a pure and innocent cowboy, led astray by the fast lady from the city." She hoped he'd rolled in cactus. Sharp, long-needled cactus. The kind that got its hooks into your flesh and never let go. "You're singing Charles Gannen's favorite song," she yelled as he collected the horses browsing a short distance off. "You cowboys are all alike."

Matthew rode over, leading Penny. Before Charlotte could mount, he corralled her between Penny and his gray gelding. "Count your lucky stars cowboys aren't all alike, cream puff. Most would have tossed you in the pond on your fancy behind for that little trick you pulled."

"Trick I pulled! Penny bumped you into the water." Charlotte met his gaze without blinking.

"I wasn't born yesterday."

"I knew you blamed me," she said in an aggrieved voice. Pushing Penny to one side, Charlotte swung up and into the saddle. "You kissed me to retaliate."

Matthew didn't deny it. "It's amazing how quickly you've overcome your fear of horses," he said instead.

Charlotte leaned down and fussed with her pant leg, straightening the trouser crease. She'd goofed in not showing fear when pressed between the two horses. "Now I've gotten to know them, I'm not afraid of Jay and Penny anymore," she finally said. "I suppose you were trying to terrorize me. More revenge?"

"Nope. Testing a theory."

She forced herself to face him. "What theory?"

"That there's more Gannen in you than you admit."

"There's none," she said flatly.

Matthew leaned over and grabbed her saddle horn, forcing Penny closer to the gelding. "As for the kiss, cream puff, those lips of yours remind me of Colorado peaches. As it happens, I'm crazy about Colorado peaches." A swat of his hand against Penny's rump sent the mare trotting across the pasture.

Charlotte considered it a miracle she hadn't toppled from the mare in complete astonishment at Matthew's comment. He couldn't possibly mean his words the way they'd sounded. Unless Matthew had an ulterior motive in saying what he'd said. He suspected she'd deliberately caused Penny to shove him in the pond. Naturally he'd pay her back. Only shoving Charlotte in the pond wasn't subtle enough for Matthew. The arrogant cowboy undoubtedly believed he was nature's gift to all womankind, and he was teasing her with the prospect of himself, much as a bratty child teases a dog with a bone. And like a bratty child, he intended to yank the bone away if Charlotte showed the least bit of interest in it. In him. Unfortunately for his clever little plan, cowboys, starting with Matthew Thorneton, left her cold. He was a fool if he thought she'd fall for such a transparent trick.

Fool he might be in some areas, but not in others. Charlotte looked at the computer screen before her. After the episode at the pond, Matthew had declared it was time to introduce her to the business side of ranching. No doubt he thought he'd be safer. Although she was surprised Matthew allowed her within shouting distance of crucial ranch records. Not that Matthew entirely trusted her. She'd spent the last two days entering information in Charles Gannen's computer, while he'd spent the days in Charles Gannen's worn leather chair, the phone practically attached to his ear as he ordered supplies and dealt with one hundred and one details. Charlotte had never dreamed ranching was such a complicated business. When Matthew spent evenings at his place catching up on paperwork, she realized it wasn't merely an excuse to get away from her. Ranching was like any other big business—tons of paperwork.

For that reason alone, Charlotte knew she could cause all sorts of mischief even with Matthew sitting across the room. She had enough experience at the store to know a myriad ways to sabotage the various files and records. If she wanted to. Matthew's thinly veiled threats delivered as he explained what he wanted done certainly wouldn't stop her. It wasn't that she was finding the information fascinating. She certainly didn't care if this cow was always a competent mother and that one always had easy births. No, she told herself, she was simply too much the businesswoman to destroy vital information.

"Am I interrupting?" Helen stood in the doorway.

Matthew signaled his mother to wait, said a few more words into the phone and hung up the receiver. "Go ahead." He leaned back and stretched his arms over his head.

"Lily called me earlier. She and Sam are having a barbecue Friday night and want us to come."

"Hell, why Friday? Sam knows I'm moving the cattle up on Saturday."

"Because Paula's home. You said yourself they never know how long she'll stay." Helen turned to Charlotte. "The Kenton place is the showcase of the county. One of Paula's husbands was something in the arts, and he talked Lily into tearing down the original 1914 ranch house. In its place they put up something Paula calls a tribute to Colorado's mining heritage. Charlotte, wait until you see Lily's kitchen. Every woman for miles around would give her eyeteeth for that kitchen."

The Kentons. Where Tim was staying. "I wouldn't want to horn in on your party. You two go without me," Charlotte said.

"Don't be silly. Of course you're coming with us. Matt's been expecting you to do too much," Helen scolded. "Riding the range, checking cattle, stringing fence—" she ignored her son's snort in the background "—and now these long hours at the computer. You've only been to Durango once since you arrived. It's time you discovered ranch life isn't all work. We play once in awhile. Sam will barbecue a cow or two and half the state will be invited. Timmy will be so disappointed if you don't go."

Before Matthew could explain to his mother exactly why Charlotte was not to attend the party, Charlotte rushed into speech. "I'm sure it will be a wonderful party, but I'd rather stay here. You and Matthew are the ones Tim will want to see."

"Matt..." his mother appealed to him.

"What Mom means, cream puff, is if you don't go, she'll feel obligated to stay home. And Mom loves a party."

"Matt! I wanted you to persuade Charlotte, not try to blackmail her into going."

"Blackmail?" Matthew lifted a quizzical brow. "I can't imagine either Charlotte or I sinking so low as to blackmail someone. Can you, Charlotte?"

"I didn't say anything about Charlotte blackmailing anyone," Helen retorted. "She's not the type to go around twisting people's arms."

Charlotte smirked across the room at Matthew. He'd better be careful or she would go to the party. He'd have to spend the entire evening trying to keep her from contaminating his son. Paula wouldn't like that.

"I bow to your superior judgment, Mom. A lady such as Charlotte would never stoop to blackmail." He folded his hands behind his head. "Persuasion, huh?" He gazed thoughtfully at Charlotte. "Let's see, cream puff, I don't believe I've introduced you to that very basic ranch chore that involves a shovel, have I? Given your choice between going to the party and cleaning the barn, what would be your choice?"

"Stop teasing her, Matt. If Charlotte doesn't want to go, she doesn't have to." Helen disappeared down the hallway.

"That was unfair, Matthew," Charlotte said immediately. "You know very well you'd break my leg before you'd let me go and breathe the same air as your son."

"Let me worry about Tim, cream puff." He stood up and grabbed his hat from the corner of the desk. "I'll be at my place the rest of the day. On my way out, I'll tell Mom you've changed your mind about going." He pulled his hat over his forehead, a mocking smile crinkling the corners of his eyes. "I can hardly wait to see what kind of party dress a lady wears to a barbecue."

If that was a challenge, Charlotte thought as she looked in the mirror Friday evening, she felt she'd met it successfully. Strawberry-blond hair tumbling around her shoulders, cream-colored off-the-shoulder blouse trimmed in antique lace, long silky rayon lavender floral skirt and—she stretched out one foot—purple, high-heeled, lace-up boots. Large-mesh purple stockings were unfortunately hidden, but maybe she'd encounter some lucky breezes at opportune moments. She giggled. Sometimes she felt as if she were acting in a very bad play. A few squirts of perfume and her grandmother's cameo on a black velvet ribbon around her neck completed her preparations. Grabbing the huge, violet-trimmed straw hat, she plopped it on her head and batted her lashes at the mirror. "Miss Prissy Voice is ready to go," she cooed. She hoped she hadn't overdone the green eyeshadow.

"Doesn't she look charming?" Helen asked Matthew as Charlotte descended the staircase.

"Thank you. You look pretty festive yourself. Both of you," Charlotte said. Coffee brown, trim-cut trousers and shirt accentuated Matthew's tall, lean physique. No silver buttons or fancy fringe for him. The leather jacket flung over one shoulder looked butter soft.

Matthew slowly inspected her. "Very nice, cream puff. Your grandmother would be proud."

The gleam of appreciation in his gaze sent a warm shiver down her spine as she followed Helen from the house. "At least we don't have to crowd into the pickup," she said, for something to say.

"A good thing," Matthew agreed, shutting the back car door of Helen's sedan as his mother settled in place. Going around the car, he opened the front passenger door for Charlotte. Helen had insisted Charlotte sit up front for better viewing. "Driving down the road with you squeezed beside me, smelling the way you do, could be downright dangerous."

Charlotte concentrated on fastening her seat belt. Remembering Matthew was only extracting revenge became more difficult with each provocative remark he uttered and each lazy, masculine smile he sent her way. Fortunately she was returning to Denver on Sunday, her two weeks dutifully served. Shifting slightly, she asked Helen about the others who'd be attending the party. Only half listening to the older woman, Charlotte gazed out the windows. Afternoon rain showers had washed the sky and decorated sagebrush with silver droplets that sparkled when touched by the last rays of the setting sun.

Paula Kenton was again in black, skintight jeans above shiny black snakeskin boots and a form-fitting black silk vest with a plunging neckline. In case anyone was missing the point, or two points, Charlotte thought dryly, the deep expanse of skin was decorated with an elaborate silver and turquoise necklace, which ended in a silver arrow strategically nestled between two tanned mounds of flesh. Silver cuffs ringed Paula's arms and turquoise weighted down her fingers. Her blond hair was swept tightly into a sleek chignon, baring ears pierced and cuffed with silver earrings. She reeked of sex appeal.

"She's not wearing a blouse," Helen said in a low, scandalized voice.

Charlotte suddenly felt as dowdy as if she were wearing one of her grandmother's housedresses. "You have to admit she looks stunning. Not many women could pull off that outfit."

Helen snorted and veered off to greet friends as Paula bore down on them.

"Matt, darling." Paula draped herself against his chest. "I thought you'd never get here."

He unfastened her clinging arms and drew Charlotte forward. "You remember Charlotte."

"Of course. Don't you look nice in your cute little cowgirl outfit."

Charlotte let that one pass. "It was so sweet of you to invite a perfect stranger." Paula didn't hold the patent on insincerity.

"Hardly a stranger," Paula said archly. "You're the talk of the town. Everyone is just dying to see Chick's long-lost illegitimate daughter."

"Tim," Matthew said in an quiet explosion of breath. "I'll wring his neck."

"It's no secret, Matthew," Charlotte said.

Paula practically danced with anticipation, her eyes glittering with dislike as she looked at Charlotte. "He was simply full of the exciting news. It's been Scarlet this and Scarlet that ever since he got here. You can imagine how stunned we all were to hear about Chick messing around in Denver all those years ago. None of us ever dreamed he'd be the type to pick up some girl off the streets. Chick, of all people, why he talked so slow, never saying much..."

Anger ripped through Charlotte's body. In a few short words Paula had attacked Jewel Darnelle's morals and Chick Gannen's intellect. Charlotte dug her fingernails painfully deep into her palms, fighting the urge to slap Paula across her nasty mouth.

Matthew laid an arm across Charlotte's shoulders. "Chick kept his mouth shut unless he had something worth saying," Matthew said in a hard-edged voice. "Unlike some people."

His words had given Charlotte time to regain her balance. Beaming blindly in Paula's direction, she pasted a wide smile on her face. "You knew Chick!" she cried. "I didn't realize... I should have, of course, you're so much older than me." Paula's face was a comic combination of outrage and shock. A choking sound came from Matthew. "When Matthew told me Chick was engaged to a local woman I didn't realize she was you. I'm so sorry, and of course, I forgive you for saying such an ugly thing about my mother, because I realize you wouldn't behave in such a childish way if Chick hadn't hurt you so badly by jilting you. Really, Paula," she added earnestly, speaking louder over the other woman's furious interjections, "you must move on and not allow what happened to blight your life, because you look great. I know a couple of old fogies, I mean, nice older men, in Denver. You mustn't think just because my mom turned them down—"

"Why, you freckle-faced bitch, how dare you?"

Charlotte looked squarely at Paula. Fury had stripped the other woman of any vestige of sex appeal. Charlotte almost felt sorry for her. "Don't ever cast slurs on my mother's character," she said quietly. "You haven't been such a success at married life yourself. You have no right to throw stones."

"At least I haven't gone around populating the world with unwanted red-haired kids," Paula sneered.

"Maybe if you'd ever loved somebody beside yourself—"

Matthew yanked Charlotte across the yard. "Are you crazy? In another second the two of you would have been rolling in the dirt, fighting."

Charlotte peeled his fingers away from her arm. "Were you worried I'd beat her up?"

"Beat her up?" He looked at her in astonishment. "You'd have been a greasy spot in the grass when she finished." After a minute, he said, "Don't judge the others here by Paula. It's who a person is and what she does that counts around here, not who her folks were," he said, his voice almost gruff. "Nobody's judging you or your mom."

"Don't worry about it. The first time someone called me names and said I couldn't come to her birthday party, I cried. Mom was devastated, but Aunt Faye was furious. With me for bawling. She told me the circumstances of my birth had nothing to do with me, and that anyone stupid enough to think they did wasn't worth knowing."

"Nice philosophy," he said skeptically, "but did it really make you feel any better?"

"No." Charlotte gave him a demure smile. "But shoving the girl in a mud puddle did."

Matthew eyed her thoughtfully. "Revenge. Mud puddle. Stock pond. I'm beginning to see a pattern here." He brushed hair from her face, then stilled, his hand cupping her jaw. "When it comes to water, I'm beginning to think you're a much more dangerous woman than I realized."

The voices and sounds of the party faded. Charlotte was aware of nothing but the warmth of Matthew's fingers against her skin and the sleepy heat in the brown

eyes fixed on her face. She fought to escape the spell he
was casting, reminding herself he only wanted something from her. "The water rights," she said breathlessly. "I suppose you're thinking about those water
rights you want."

"I'm thinking if a man weren't careful, he could drown
in green eyes."

CHAPTER NINE

CHARLOTTE blinked uncertainly at the soft, teasing words, clear thinking hindered by Matthew caressing her jawbone with his thumb. Understanding finally dawned. Matthew's flirting was his way of erasing the echoes of Paula Kenton's ugly, spiteful remarks. Charlotte swallowed the lump of gratitude in her throat and rewarded him with an incandescent smile. "Do you flirt with every female who crosses your path?"

"Most of the females who cross my path are big and ugly and chew their cuds. Not my type."

"Since you're a cowboy, seems to me they'd be exactly your type," Charlotte retorted. Smiling golden brown eyes wouldn't affect her breathing, so it must be the altitude. Were they higher or lower here than in Denver? Could the altitude be the cause of the electric tension buzzing between them? She felt invigorated and recharged and full of nervous energy. At the same time she wished she could curl her entire body into a small ball that would fit in Matthew's hand.

"I thought you guys was never gonna get here."

The shrill voice rescued Charlotte, and she turned and smiled gratefully at Tim. "I suppose you want to know how that repellent animal you stuck me with baby-sitting is."

"Dad told me you take good care of Snowball." Tim's smile disappeared, and he formally added, "I'm sorry about your hat. Dad says I have to buy you a new one."

"He told you that? He told me anyone who put a hat with fake cherries on it right beside a rat's cage deserved to have it gnawed on. Before you ask, Snowball didn't get sick.''

"Gosh, Charlotte. I wasn't going to ask that."

"Why not? Your dad already tell you he's OK?"

"Yeah." Tim gave her an enchanting grin.

Charlotte barely restrained herself from hugging him. As an only child, she'd always wanted a younger brother or sister. No wonder she'd fallen in love with Tim. Except Tim was off limits to her. By decree of Matthew. She pushed the sad knowledge away. "You didn't warn me Snowball likes tea," she said in a severe voice.

Tim's face lit up with delight. "Only Earl Grey," he crowed. "Dad told me he climbed in your mug, and you didn't see him till you picked it up."

Charlotte gave him a fierce frown. "You're lucky I didn't bite him, kiddo. Don't you believe me?" she asked as Tim erupted in giggles.

"Nah. You like him. Dad said you got him in your room so he won't get lonely." Tim grabbed her hand. "C'mon. I want to show you to my friends."

Charlotte looked at Matthew. He'd stood quietly during her conversation with his son, but she had no doubt he'd intervene before allowing her to accompany Tim. To her surprise, Matthew raised no objection.

"Go ahead, there's some people I want to talk to. Tim," Matthew instructed his son, "introduce Charlotte to your grandparents."

Charlotte was involved in a fierce game of croquet with a mixed group of children and adults when Matthew came looking for her. Tim trotted over to his dad. "Charlotte says I knock her out again and she's gonna throw a temper tantrum."

"In that case, it's a good thing I've come to take her away." Matthew tousled his son's hair.

The affectionate gesture brought a lump to Charlotte's throat as Tim rushed to assure his father Charlotte was only teasing.

"I know, but there's someone here who wants to meet her."

The man's name was Bud Adamly. "I couldn't believe it when Matt told me you were Chick's daughter. I mean, I believe it," he added hastily, "it's just, well, hell, I'm pleased as punch Chick had a kid."

"Chick occasionally hazed for Bud," Matthew said.

"That's right. The last time I saw your father was in Denver at the stock show just before he left for Vietnam." The man scrutinized Charlotte's face. "You sure look like Emily, Chick's mother. Course you have Jewel's smile."

"My mother's..." Charlotte's voice caught in her throat.

"The way she looked at Chick you'd have thought he was a million-dollar pile of gold. I envied him, I'll tell you that. I'll bet she's still pretty as a picture."

"You met my mother?"

"Sure. Chick introduced her to me. I admit, I wondered, what with Connie and—" He broke off, his face dark red.

"Charlotte knows about Connie," Matthew said.

"Chick may have been engaged to Connie, but I never saw him as happy as he was with your mom. When I heard Chick was killed, I felt better knowing he'd had those days with Jewel. I liked her. In fact—" his face lit up "—you tell her to come down and visit us. My wife and I, we'd love to have her. Show her around, where Chick went to school, stuff like that."

Charlotte could do little more than nod as Bud Adamly said his farewells and walked away. She had no idea how her hand came to be tightly clasped in Matthew's, but she was grateful for his support. "Thank you," she managed.

Matthew wiped a spot of moisture from her cheek. "Bud is pretty sure your dad was riding Willie that time."

"Willie." Matthew hadn't forgotten. She was still shamelessly clutching his hand when her hard-won composure dissolved into high-pitched giggles. "Willie. What a ridiculous name for a horse. Satan, or Thor, or Chief, but Willie?"

"I think you need something to eat," Matthew said.

Charlotte wondered if she could smell the fried chicken from the rear of the pickup, or if after several hours of preparing the enormous picnic lunch, the odor was in her head. "You must be feeding an army," she said to Helen, who was driving.

"The men started out before light, so they'll be starving. I know you were annoyed with Matt for not letting you go along today, but I really appreciate your help."

So Helen had overheard last evening's shouted argument. "I would not have needed baby-sitting." Charlotte still nursed her grievance, conveniently forgetting whose behavior had provided the excuse Matthew needed. He'd claimed her riding skills weren't up to the challenge of the drive. "He let Tim go." She knew very well Tim's presence on the drive was why she'd been banished to the kitchen, not because she was a greenhorn.

Helen wisely changed the subject as she brought the pickup to a halt. "Good. We beat them here. They're just coming through the far gate."

Charlotte twisted around in her seat. Cattle were streaming from one field to another. A rider sat by the opened gate, while a half dozen other riders walked and trotted the outskirts of the plodding herd. The sounds of the herd were punctuated by shouts of the riders. The cows looked hot and tired, their bovine hooves kicking up a cloud of dust. One cow dashed from the herd, headed away from the gate. A rider dashed after, swinging a large loop. The cow changed direction, but the horse whirled on his back legs, cutting the cow off from freedom. Obediently the cow trotted back to the herd. The gray horse and rider swung to the rear of the herd.

"Matt trained Jay himself," Helen said proudly. "He's one of the best cutting horses I've ever seen. Matt's been offered big money for Jay, but he won't sell." Her voice changed. "Oh, darn. Why is she along?"

She was Paula Kenton. Matthew had allowed her to join the drive. Maybe he didn't dislike Paula as much as he claimed. Charlotte took quiet satisfaction in the other woman's sweat-stained clothes, dust-caked face and hair plastered to her head.

Naturally Paula was less than pleased by the unflattering contrast. "Too bad you wouldn't ride with us today, Carla. Matt and I commented on how particularly gorgeous the sunrise was this morning. Of course, I understand you needing your beauty sleep." She poked around the platter of chicken. "City folk never fully appreciate the beauty of nature, anyway."

Charlotte gave Matthew an indignant look. She'd bet Paula hadn't reached those conclusions unaided.

"I asked Charlotte to help Mom out today, and although she preferred to ride, she graciously—" Matthew's eyes gleamed with laughter across the makeshift serving table at Charlotte "—consented. The men and I can handle the drive without outside help, but we'd never survive without a good lunch."

Paula surveyed Charlotte through contemptuous eyes, taking in every detail of the huge straw hat, the finely tucked almond-colored high-necked blouse with an old Victorian pin at the collar, and the coral chintz skirt. "I'll bet she was a big help. Is there anything at all you can do in the kitchen?"

Charlotte winked at Tim, who was in line ahead of his dad. "I managed to lick the beaters after Helen mixed up the chocolate frosting." She swallowed a smile as Tim screwed up his face to wink back. Out of the corner of her eye she saw Matthew watching the byplay. She didn't care. She was leaving tomorrow.

"Charlotte's the best cutter-upper and cleanup crew I've ever had," Helen said stoutly.

"Lara always went with the men on the drive," Paula said. "She believed a woman should be able to work alongside her man, and she was a better rider and cowhand than most of the men."

"Yes, she was," Matthew agreed in a pleasant voice. "You forgot to take carrots and potato salad, Tim. A cowboy can't make it through the day on chicken and cake."

"The boy's diet is deplorable," Paula said immediately. "Mom and Dad let him eat all kinds of junk food, and I suppose you're not much better, Helen. He needs a mother."

A calf bawled in the sudden silence. Tim reached for a carrot stick, his face pale. Charlotte was torn between an angry urge to throw the entire bowl of potato salad at Paula, and a sense of astonishment that Paula had so little sense when it came to dealing with Matthew. Had Lara been as inept? If so, it was hardly surprising they'd come to a parting of the ways.

"Mom, you and Charlotte better fill your plates before the men come back for seconds or you'll go away hungry." Matthew joined the cowhands sitting in the shade of some large pines. Paula pointedly sat down beside him.

Helen indicated the two lawn chairs she'd set up in the shade of the truck. "No point in you and me getting all dirty."

Tim dropped to the ground between them, his resentful gaze on Paula as she whispered in Matthew's ear. Charlotte resisted the temptation to assure Tim his father was safe from Paula. What did she know? Matthew ate steadily, his face blank. The men returned for second and third helpings and then most of them, including Matthew, stretched out on the ground, hats covering their faces. Tim curled up in a ball on the ground, and even Helen sat with her eyes closed. Paula had disappeared.

Loud snores came from under one of the hats, and Charlotte idly wondered if Matthew snored. Cattle sounds drifted from the pasture, and a few insects buzzed halfheartedly in the midday warmth. Across the road a cool fringe of trees beckoned. Moving quietly, Charlotte stood up and strolled toward the trees. A dark blue Steller's jay squawked at her intrusion, and a squirrel scolded from overhead.

"If you think you can get to Matt by cozying up to his precious son, it won't work." Paula stepped from behind a large tree. "You don't fit in here with your fancy clothes and soft city ways, and you never will. Especially after Lara. A woman like you might be good for sex—" Paula looked doubtful "—but Matt will no more marry you than Chick married your mother."

Without a word, Charlotte executed a U-turn and returned to her lawn chair. As much as she wanted to pound the other woman into the ground, she would not stoop to Paula's level and engage in a cat fight. Paula knew nothing about Jewel Darnelle. If Chick Gannen wouldn't have married her, it was because he was stupid. His decision had nothing to do with her mother's worth.

"What did Paula say?" Helen asked later as they drove to the ranch house. "The way you came shooting out of those trees, at first I thought a bear was after you."

Charlotte was more interested in Paula's sister. "What was Lara like?"

"Don't judge her by Paula. She was lively, but kind. And hardworking. Matt started dating her when he was fifteen and she was fourteen. Matt went off to Colorado State University and Lara followed him a year later. They married after her first year of school, and Tim arrived two weeks after Matt graduated. They were the perfect couple, ranch kids who knew what they wanted, and deeply in love. I ran the ranch, with Matt helping during vacations, until Matt and Lara came back. I relied heavily on Charlie after my first husband died, and marrying Charlie seemed the right thing to do. Maybe I should have waited awhile, not been so anxious to leave Lara and Matt on their own. Matt was so determined to prove himself, he worked twenty-four hours a day. If I'd stayed, I could have watched Tim, and Lara could have been out on a horse, working right beside Matt." A light rain began falling, and Helen switched on the windshield wipers. "When I saw them together, they seemed happy. I didn't realize... Matt blames himself."

"Matthew told me she was killed," Charlotte said.

"A movie company was here making a Western. They wanted locals who could ride. On a lark, Lara signed up." Helen squinted into the increasing rain. "I hope we make it home before this gets worse," she said absently, before returning to the subject of Lara. "She was beautiful and when she rode her mare, the two of them were a sight to see. Everyone noticed Lara, made over her.''

''So she went to Hollywood to be a movie star,'' Charlotte guessed.

''She felt like life had passed her by. Dating only Matt, marrying so early... Matt had no idea she was bored and unhappy. They made an agreement. She'd give Hollywood a try for one year, coming home at least twice a month. Matt and Tim moved in with Charlie and me. Matt thought she'd discover Hollywood was full of beautiful women and come home.'' Helen's voice flattened. ''She'd been out there three weeks when she was shot. She died on the way to the hospital.''

''Poor Matthew. He must miss her very much.''

''Yes.'' Helen hunched over the steering wheel. Lightning flashed to their right. ''Paula's right about one thing. He should get married again. Not for Timmy, but... Matt's still a young man. I don't believe in locking up hearts. I loved Matt's dad, but I found happiness with Charlie, too, even if he was a cantankerous old buzzard.''

''I don't imagine many women would want to compete with the memory of a beautiful, dashing young wife,'' Charlotte said.

''Nonsense. Don't let your mother's example sway you into thinking a person can only fall in love once in a lifetime.'' Helen turned to face Charlotte earnestly across the bench seat. ''Sure, Matt loved Lara, but that's the past. Matt has plenty of love left in him for a second wife. Don't you worry about that.''

Before Charlotte could point out her lack of interest in Matthew's ability to love a second wife, Helen's split second of inattention allowed the pickup to develop a mind of its own. The vehicle slid inexorably to the side of the road in spite of the older woman's best efforts. "Darn gumbo," Helen said grimly.

Before Charlotte could ask what gumbo was, the vehicle slipped off the road and jarred and jolted its way down a short but steep incline, Helen fighting the wheel. Charlotte stared in horror, praying they'd reach bottom without meeting total disaster. Just when it appeared her prayers would be answered, a small, insignificant bush proved to be obstacle enough to flip the pickup. The landscape whirled by in a tumbling kaleidoscope of green and brown and blue, yet at the same time they seemed to be rolling over in slow motion, with Charlotte aware of the scent of damp sage, the smell of ozone, a bird fluttering up from a bush. She thought she was screaming. The pickup bounced to a stop, shuddered and then slowly settled upright on its tires.

The window beside Charlotte had shattered, and pieces of glass lay in her lap. The front windshield was gone, and cold rain poured in. For an moment she sat stunned, then a single thought roused her. "Fuel tanks. We have to get out of the truck. In case it blows up." Helen looked blank. Charlotte's door was jammed shut. Reaching over, she unbelted Helen's seat belt, breathing a sigh of relief when Helen's door opened at a push. She couldn't shove the older woman out of the truck when she didn't know the extent of her injuries. Snaking out through the open windshield onto the hood of the pickup, Charlotte jumped to the ground and hastened to help Helen from the vehicle. Helen was still dazed, but Charlotte managed to half-carry and half-drag her to what she judged a safe distance from the truck. Lowering the older woman to the ground, Charlotte dropped beside her. "Are you OK?" she asked Helen anxiously.

Helen slowly shook her head. "I think I must have hit my head and blacked out for a minute." Helen shivered. "Charlotte, I'm so sorry."

In the movies wrecked cars always seemed to explode, but there was no sign of fire around the truck. Charlotte had no idea if it was safe to return to the vehicle. Not that the windowless pickup would keep them much dryer, and she doubted the crumpled truck was drivable. The words Helen had said just prior to the accident came back to her. "What is gumbo?"

"When the dirt around here gets wet, we call it gumbo. It's slicker than grease. I've driven on it enough, we'd have been OK if I'd been paying attention to my driving."

"It was my fault," Charlotte said. "Distracting you with questions. What do we do now? How long do you think it will be before Matthew or one of the hands comes along?"

Helen winced. "They'll be coming from the north pasture, not from where we had lunch. I'm afraid they'll be taking the other road."

The rain had eased up, only a few drops falling around them. "I guess we better start hiking," Charlotte said.

"I'm sorry, but—" Helen look a deep breath "—I don't think I can. I'm afraid I've dislocated my shoulder, and unless you know how to pop it back in—" she managed a smile at Charlotte's horrified disclaimer "—I don't think I'm going anywhere."

"You must be in agony, and here I manhandled you out of the truck. I didn't do it then, did I?"

"No. I bounced off the door when the pickup rolled. I'll be all right as soon as it's popped back. Meanwhile—" Helen made a face "—we'll have to wait here. We're still about ten miles from the ranch."

Ten miles. Charlotte's heart sank. Still, there was a road. "I'll start hiking and hope someone comes along."

"Unfortunately, this road doesn't see much traffic, so you might have to walk all the way." Helen looked at Charlotte's feet. "It would probably be best if you waited here. Matt will come looking for us when he gets home, and I'll be fine until he finds us."

Charlotte wanted desperately to believe Helen felt only the barest twinge of pain, but she could read the suffering etched on the older woman's face. She wished she could believe Matthew would find them soon, but chances were Matthew would hang around the Kentons' for dinner and until Tim went to bed. Wet and chilled, Helen was a candidate for pneumonia. There was only one answer to their problem. Charlotte had to hoof it. She looked ruefully at the sandals that had caught Helen's doubtful gaze. At least they were flat sandals, not the three-inch-high heels she'd contemplated wearing.

Leaving Helen as dry and comfortable as possible with a tarp, a plastic tablecloth and some drinking water gingerly retrieved from the pickup, Charlotte scrambled up the rocky, slick incline, slipping back two steps for every forward step she managed. Bidding Helen a cheery farewell, she set off briskly down the road, carrying water in a bottle she'd found in the pickup.

After what seemed an eternity of walking, Charlotte was reduced to concentrating on moving first one foot and then the other. Dusk had come and gone, and a star-studded sky and black lace clouds over a partial moon held little charm. Her eyes had adjusted to the semi-darkness, but the road was slick and rutted and she'd lost track of the number of times she'd tripped and fallen. Half the gumbo in the state of Colorado must be plastered to her. The last time she'd picked herself up, Charlotte had decided to heck with bears and mountain lions and rustlers and snakes and whatever else lurked in the brush. She no longer had the energy to run in panic at every looming shadow and frightening sound.

Plodding along, her labored breathing echoing loudly in her ears, at first Charlotte paid no attention to the sound of an approaching vehicle. When the noise registered, she moved to one side of the road and waved her arms and shouted. The dark pickup braked to an abrupt stop. Matthew erupted from the driver's side. Charlotte sank wearily to the ground. "It's about time."

"What happened?" Rushing to her, Matthew lifted Charlotte from the ground and carried her to the pickup. "Where's Mom?"

"Back that way." Charlotte brushed her hair away from her face with a muddy hand. "We had a little accident, and she thinks she dislocated her shoulder. We have to go get her."

"We will." Matthew grabbed a jacket from behind his seat, tucked it around Charlotte and fastened her seat belt, scrutinizing her face in the pickup's interior light. His eyes narrowed and he reached up and gently touched her cheek. "Blood. Yours or Mom's?" he asked roughly.

"I don't know. There was broken glass, but I'm OK." She gave him a tired smile. "I'm afraid I have more than a little smudge on my dress, and I'm sure I chipped my toenail polish."

Matthew's lips tightened and he turned the key with a hard, impatient gesture. "Can you show me where Mom is?"

"I think so. I put a white food cooler beside the road in case we couldn't see the truck." If Matthew had any idea how many times she'd tripped and fallen hauling the awkward cooler up to the road, his contempt for her would only deepen. Obviously he'd taken seriously her attempts at humor. Now she was safe, Charlotte had difficulty controlling her shivers. Tears hovered near the surface, but she refused to burst out bawling. Matthew already believed her silly and weak. The little game she'd been playing on him no longer seemed so amusing.

The distance that had taken her eons to walk was quickly covered by the pickup, and in no time at all, the cooler showed up white in the headlights. "There it is," Matthew said. "Good work." Then he was out of the truck and plunging down the side of the ravine.

Hearing Helen's voice, Charlotte sagged weakly against the back of the seat, only now willing to admit how scared she'd been that leaving Helen might have been the wrong decision. Head injuries could have frightening consequences, and more than once along the road the fear had surfaced that Helen might have been suffering from a heart attack instead of a dislocated shoulder. At any rate, exhausted as Charlotte was, Helen was the one needing medical attention. Wearily Charlotte climbed out of the pickup as Matthew carried his mother up to the road. His easy ascent made a mockery of the struggles Charlotte had had earlier climbing the same incline.

Matthew carefully settled his mother in the middle of the seat and fastened her seat belt. "OK?"

"I don't need to see a doctor," Helen protested. "You or Dennis can pop it back into place."

Charlotte had the feeling Helen had been arguing this particular point since Matthew had climbed down to her. Scrambling into the pickup, Charlotte took Helen's cold hand in hers and gently chafed it in an effort to restore some warmth. "Did you think I'd never get back?"

"It was a long wait," Helen admitted. "I passed the time by swearing at Charlie. Told him if he hadn't been such an ornery, stubborn old coot, you wouldn't have grown up wearing party clothes to a cattle drive. I worried about you in those shoes."

"I am personally going to burn every stitch on her body," Matthew growled, "starting with those damned shoes. Of all the stupid..." He punctuated his opinion with a few curses.

Fortunately the dark hid from Matthew the sudden, hot tears cascading down Charlotte's cheeks. Matthew's opinion of her didn't mean a thing. She was just so very tired. She should have anticipated that, once at the clinic, he would immediately spot the tear tracks down her mud-splattered face and demand to know the cause. Without waiting for an answer, he'd bundled her in for her share of medical attention.

Hours later Charlotte sat wearily on the side of her bed, attempting to summon the energy to take a bath. Her extremities had been scrubbed and treated by medical personnel, but she still felt as if she'd been wallowing in a mud puddle. Her eyes closed. She'd run the water in the tub in a minute.

"Mom's settled. You're next. You'll sleep better after a nice hot bath."

Charlotte didn't bother to open her eyes. "Go away."

"I put lots of the bubble stuff I got Grandma for Christmas in for you."

Her eyelids flew up. "Where'd you come from?"

"I was with Dad, and when you wasn't here, I stayed to answer the phone. In case you called." Tim gave her a shame-faced look. "I fell asleep on the sofa after Dad called, and I didn't hear you get home. Dad said you was OK."

Charlotte dredged up a smile. "Just tired." Conscious of Matthew leaning against the doorjamb, she added, "My idea of hiking is walking to my car in the mall parking lot."

"Dad says you're a hero."

Charlotte's astonished gaze flew to Matthew. He gave her a crooked grin. "Tim's translation."

She refused to ask his actual words. Turning to Tim, she thanked him for fixing her bath.

"Dad done it. I put in the bubbles."

"OK," Matthew interposed, "you've seen for yourself that your grandmother and Charlotte are OK, so hit the sack."

"Aw, Dad..." At his father's steady look, Tim disappeared down the hall.

"I'm surprised you allowed him to return while I'm still around," Charlotte said.

"Paula is spending the night at her folks', so he didn't want to stay there."

"I thought she was staying with them."

Matthew shook his head. "She drops in occasionally, but she has an apartment in town where she spends most of her time." He straightened up. "Your bathwater is getting cold. Get moving." He wiggled his eyebrows. "If you're too tired, I'll be happy to help you off with your clothes and scrub your back."

Charlotte struggled to her feet. "I can manage."

Lowering herself into the heavenly bathwater, she smiled at the overpowering scent. Tim had poured in the bubble bath with a liberal hand. It was odd Matthew had brought his son to the ranch. Even odder he was allowing Tim to view her as having done anything heroic. Helen had thanked Charlotte profusely for her help, but Charlotte had the distinct impression she'd fallen way short of Matthew's standards. No doubt Lara would have fixed Helen's shoulder and then jogged cross-country to town bearing Helen on her back. Charlotte held one foot above the bubbles and surveyed her poor, scratched toes. In the process of the rescue Lara would have snapped heads off rattlesnakes and wrestled grizzly bears. Charlotte decided she would have intensely disliked Lara, perfect paragon that Matthew's wife had been. Even Helen sang her praises. One would think Matthew's mother would harbor a little resentment against the woman who'd abandoned Helen's son and grandson.

Not that Charlotte blamed Lara for walking out on Matthew. He'd probably carped and criticized her every waking moment. Look at the way he'd... Charlotte moved restlessly in the water. Well, actually, he hadn't criticized her excessively. In fact, he'd been remarkably patient and nonjudgmental, considering her behavior. Only because he didn't want to alienate Charlotte before he secured his precious water rights. He'd probably only filled the tub for her because he intended to ensure her health until she'd sold him what he wanted. It was a miracle he hadn't insisted on barging in here and taking care of her bath.

If he'd wanted to scrub Lara's back, he wouldn't have taken no for an answer. Well, she wasn't Lara, was she? Charlotte thought of the other woman's striking blond beauty, Lara's suitability to be Matthew's wife and the loving look on Matthew's face in their wedding picture. No, Charlotte was definitely not Lara. Not that she'd ever want to be.

"How you doing in there? Need any help?"

Charlotte jerked upright as Matthew's voice came from the other side of the door. "Don't you dare come in here!"

He chuckled. "I thought that would wake you up. Come on, get out of the tub before you fall asleep and turn into a freckled prune."

The amusement in Matthew's voice and his choice of words made it clear he considered Charlotte the same

old useless pest he'd thought her from the beginning.
She pulled the tub's plug, and the water gurgled noisily
down the drain. "I'm out. Go away." His footsteps
moved down the hall. Charlotte stepped from the tub,
toweled herself off, put on a silk nightgown and wrapped
her heavy flannel robe snugly around her. After twisting
the towel turban-style over her hair, she straightened up
the bathroom. In her bedroom her bundle of filthy
clothes fell to the floor. Most were beyond salvation.

"I'll be damned, cream puff. I could swear that thing
you're wearing is flannel."

Charlotte whipped around. "What are you doing in
here?"

Matthew lay at ease on her bed, her pillows piled beneath his head, his feet propped on the footboard of the
bed. "Making sure Tim's little heroine is safely tucked
into bed." He gave her a slow smile. "You know you're
dying to ask. Go ahead."

"I have no idea what you're talking about," she lied.
Turning her back squarely to him, she sat at the dressing
table and reached for her face cream.

"Since you asked in such a nice prissy voice..." He
grinned at her reflection in the mirror. "I told Tim you
didn't panic but helped Mom from the pickup, made her
comfortable and went for help. I told him you used your
head and marked the road to help us find Mom. I told
him you were alone in a strange place on a dark night
and were probably scared to death and you were
scratched, cut, bruised and covered with mud, but you
didn't quit." He folded his arms behind his head, his
gaze never leaving hers. "And I told him you'd walked
over eight miles wearing the worst shoes for walking man
ever devised, and you were exhausted and your legs had
probably long ago turned to rubber, but you kept on
going. To Tim, that makes you a hero."

Charlotte stared speechlessly at his image in the mirror. He must be joking.

Matthew stood and walked over to her. He rested his hands on her shoulders, his eyes holding hers in the mirror. "Thank you, Charlotte. I'm in your debt."

"I didn't do anything. You were looking for us before I ever reached the ranch."

"You helped Mom, and you saved us a lot of time searching."

Tim burst through her door. "Dad, I got a great idea. Why don't you marry Charlotte and she can stay here?"

"Sure. Why not? What do you think, Charlotte?"

CHAPTER TEN

"WHAT do you think, Charlotte?" Over a week later the words still reverberated furiously inside Charlotte's head. What did she think? She thought a herd of cattle stampeding over Matthew Thorneton's body was too agreeable a fate for him. She thought dropping him in a hole with one hundred angry rattlesnakes would be treating him too kindly. Most of all, she thought she'd be much happier, in fact ecstatic, if she'd thrown everything on her dressing table at him instead of staring stupidly at him and stammering out an idiotically polite refusal of his offhand proposal.

Charlotte slammed her fist down on the stapler, fastening several invoices together. Too bad Matthew's head wasn't between the papers. Not for the first time she told herself she should have accepted his proposal. To see the look on his face.

Of course, he would have been prepared for that. One thing living practically in Matthew's pocket for two weeks had taught her was that little took him by surprise. In the split second between Tim's artless suggestion and Matthew's agreement, Matthew might have concluded the idea had merit.

Thinking logically about her qualifications, Charlotte could come up with several reasons Matthew might marry her. Matthew admitted he needed a wife for his son. She and Tim liked each other, which, as much as she detested the scum bag, she knew would matter to Matthew. Matthew didn't love Charlotte or even particularly approve of her, but he had a man's needs, and she didn't think he'd be averse to meeting those needs in her bed. "Fat chance!" she muttered, wielding her eraser. Two plus two did not equal six. Fortunately it didn't take a mathematical genius to add up her other considerable asset—one ranch with a house, some outbuildings, a few acres and this and that. This and that including the water rights Matthew admitted he'd go to any lengths to obtain. He'd probably convinced himself he'd be doing Charlotte a favor by marrying her. She'd retain, at least symbolically—as if he'd allow her to make one tiny little decision—the Gannen family ranch, which he'd never been convinced she wanted no part of. Matthew Thorneton was stupid enough to think marrying her would compensate for the way Jewel had been treated by Charles and Chick Gannen.

Charlotte wished a customer would come into Romance and Old Lace so she had less time to dwell on things she'd rather forget. Such as Matthew driving her to the airport the day after his astonishing proposal and never mentioning it. Such as the offer to buy the Gannen property, which had arrived yesterday in the mail. Charlotte hadn't bothered to read it. She had no intention of haggling over price. She simply wanted the ranch, the Gannens and Matthew Thorneton out of her life.

"Charlotte?"

The hesitant voice from the other side of the counter startled her. She hadn't heard anyone come in. Her gaze flew to a spot above Tim's head. No one stood there. Charlotte looked down. "This is a surprise. Where's your dad?"

He shrugged. "I hafta go to the bathroom."

Troubled by the evasive answer, Charlotte counseled herself to be patient. The mall restrooms were only a few feet away, and she stood in the doorway to the store waiting for Tim to return. "Now. Where's your dad?"

Tim checked the price tag on a straw hat. "Jeez. No wonder you was mad at Snowball for eating yours."

"I wasn't mad." Tim's obvious reluctance to answer her question occasioned a sense of foreboding, but she refused to panic. He could be embarrassed after her refusal to marry his dad. "Are you with your grandmother?" At his quick head shake, she asked, "With your Kenton grandparents? Your aunt Paula?" Each question prompted another negative shake. He was avoiding her eyes. "Timothy Thorneton," she said sternly. That won her a quick, narrow-eyed look of reproach. "What's going on?"

Tim ran a finger down the glass showcase. "Dad told Grandma he's buying your ranch. He said you didn't want it." He looked at Charlotte, hurt and censure spilling from his eyes. "Me and Snowball thought you liked us."

Charlotte walked around the showcase. "It has nothing to do with you," she began, reaching for Tim's stiff shoulders.

He shrugged off her hands. "Why won't you marry Dad? Now he's gonna marry her and I hate you."

Judging from the pain, her heart had shattered into a million pieces. She managed to gather herself raggedly together. She had to deal with Tim. She'd deal with the rest later. "You ran away from home, didn't you?" At his nod, she sighed, brushed aside some clothing from a wicker chair and sat so her eyes were level with his. "You better tell me about it." When he finished she said, "I have to call your dad. He must be frantic."

"I wouldn't run away if you married him."

Charlotte shook her head. "That's baby talk. You can't go around hurting and scaring people who love you just to get your own way."

Tim hung his head and scuffed his toe along the pattern of the rug. "You mad at me? Don't you like me no more?"

Charlotte held out her arms. As Tim gripped her neck tightly, she breathed in the smell of small boy and blinked back hot tears. "Hey, kiddo, we'll always be friends."

"I don't hate you."

"I know." Charlotte gave him one last squeeze and dialed the ranch. Matthew answered the phone. "Matthew, it's Charlotte. I—"

"I can't talk right now. I don't want to tie up the phone. Tim—"

"Is here." Dead silence greeted her words. "In Denver. He remembered the name of the mall and—"

"I'll charter a plane and be there as soon as I can," came Matthew's grim voice.

"I'm closing early and taking him home right now. Matthew, he's fine."

"So far." He slammed the phone down.

"Is he mad?" The freckles stood out on Tim's wan face.

"Maybe a little. He must have been terribly worried."

Tim gave her a speculative look. "He'll probably beat me."

"Timothy Thorneton, I don't believe your father has ever beaten you or ever would."

"Once me and my friend was messing around and Dennis's chickens sorta got loose. Dad made me catch them and I had to get the eggs and clean the henhouse. For a whole week."

Charlotte had a hard time not laughing at the outrage in Tim's voice.

* * *

Everyone else had gone to bed by the time Matthew's pounding fist summoned Charlotte to the door. Not bothering to acknowledge her, he strode into the house. "Where is he?"

"Upstairs, in my room, sleeping."

Matthew brushed past her, covering the entry in one stride. He started up the stairs two at a time.

"Matthew, wait."

He stopped and turned. "What's wrong?"

"Tim's fine, really." Charlotte grabbed the newel post at the bottom of the staircase. "I just thought... He's only a little boy. Maybe you should wait until morning and..." Her voice withered under Matthew's blistering look as he moved slowly down the stairs until he towered over her.

He grabbed her face, forcing her to look at him. "Are you trying to protect my son from me?" he asked savagely. "Did he say he needed your protection?"

His fingers were crushing her chin. "I know you're angry, and—"

"Why should I be angry? My son ran away from home rather than come to me with whatever problem he had. And you're acting as if I routinely take a belt to him." His fingers tightened. "Lara never came to me with her unhappiness, either. What kind of uncaring monster do you all think I am?"

The pain of Matthew's fierce grip was nothing compared to the suffering he was inflicting on himself. His voice might sound thick with rage, but bewilderment and hurt darkened his brown eyes. "I'm sorry," she said. "I'm acting like an idiot. I know you're not going to harm him." Reaching up, she pressed her fingers lightly against Matthew's cheek. "As for Tim, I think having to clean Dennis's chicken coop is what worries him most."

Matthew frowned at her, then uttered a sharp bark of laughter. He eased the pressure on her chin. "He tell you why?"

She nodded. "Go see for yourself he's OK, and then I'll tell you what he told me. Second door on the right."

Matthew absently dropped a quick kiss on her lips before racing up the staircase. When he returned, Charlotte handed him coffee in a mug she'd unearthed from the back of a cupboard. He took a deep swallow. "Thanks. I didn't take time for dinner." She lifted a napkin off a plate of sandwiches. Grabbing one, Matthew took a large bite and saluted her with the rest of the sandwich. Eventually he put down the empty plate and leaned his head back against the sofa, stretching out his long legs and closing his eyes.

Charlotte allowed her gaze to roam freely over him. Matthew had obviously rushed to the airport without changing, his work boots covered with who-knew-what and a smear of mud decorating his worn jeans. He'd tossed his dirty, battered cowboy hat on the table and his hair was a mess. Deep squint lines fanned out from his closed eyes, while a patch of windburn reddened one cheek. He needed a shave. Even with eyelashes long and dark against tanned skin, Matthew could not precisely be called handsome. What he was was devastatingly male.

"Interesting bedroom you have."

Busy telling herself Matthew's masculine charms meant nothing to her, it took a moment before his words penetrated. It had been foolish to hope he'd be too distracted to notice the various photographs and ribbons hanging on her bedroom walls. Nothing escaped Matthew's keen eyes. "So now you know."

"I knew before. The second night you were at the ranch, I called your mom to assure her I hadn't strangled you yet.'' He opened one eye. ''She was pleased to hear you'd been riding, and went on at great length about your horseback riding experience and skills. I assume you didn't tell her of your plans because she wouldn't have approved.''

''Why didn't you say something?''

''You didn't seem to be doing any real harm, and I hated to spoil your fun. And I didn't want to spoil mine,'' he added unexpectedly, grinning slightly. ''You were as entertaining as a TV comedy. I never knew what you were going to think of next.''

''You weren't so amused when you landed in the stock pond.''

''Ah, the stock pond.'' He straightened up. ''Tell me why Tim ran away.'' The hint of laughter disappeared from his voice. His face was grim, almost haggard.

''He didn't really run away,'' Charlotte said quickly. ''He wanted to talk to me, and a high school boy, the brother of a friend, was driving up, and Tim convinced the boy he had your permission to come.''

''Why you?''

His unblinking stare unnerved her. Not that she'd expected this discussion to be easy. Charlotte stared at the wallpaper behind his head. ''He found out you're going to marry Paula.''

''How he'd find that out?''

So it was true. The lights in the living room momentarily dimmed. She folded her hands in her lap. ''Paula told him.''

''I still don't understand why he came to you.''

''He wanted me to tell you I'd changed my mind,'' she said evenly. ''To tell you I'd marry you.''

His gaze never left her face. ''What did you tell him?''

''I said you'd never marry Paula.''

''Did he believe you?''

"No. Paula's parents told him it was true, and he saw they were excited about it. When he went to ask your mom, he found her unpacking an old wedding dress, for the bride, she said. She was so happy, he didn't tell her he hated the idea."

"Why didn't he ask me?"

"He said he did, and you told him it was a big secret and you thought it best not to talk about it yet."

"Ah." Matthew lounged back against the sofa. "I remember that conversation. I also remember thinking at the time his reception of the news wasn't quite what I'd anticipated, but I assumed it was a passing pang of jealousy. The child suddenly realizing he'll have to share the parent. That sort of thing."

Charlotte sprang to her feet and paced across the rug. "Matthew, you know Tim detests Paula and she detests him."

"I don't think I'd put it quite so strongly."

She whirled, her hands on her hips. "How would you put it when a woman refuses to call her future stepson by his name?"

Matthew shrugged. "Things will work out."

"Sure. She'll probably send him off to boarding school," Charlotte snapped.

"I'm not sure it's your concern."

The tone was mild, but the words were a slap across her face. "I like Tim," she said stiffly. "I care about his happiness and well-being."

"If you really care—" Matthew's gaze followed her agitated pacing across the floor "—you'll do something about it."

Charlotte turned slowly to face him. If she'd misunderstood the challenge in his words, there was no misunderstanding the challenge clearly written on his face.

She cleared her throat. "Such as what?" she asked, her voice barely above a whisper.

His gaze bore steadily into hers. "What Tim said. Marry me. Save me from Paula."

A million inner voices screamed at her to turn him down. "All right. I will marry you." The minute the words were out of her mouth she wanted desperately to recall them. The odd look on his face brought it forcibly home to her he'd clearly expected her to say no. Not knowing how to retreat, she plunged ahead. "But I'll want a prenuptial agreement."

Matthew had regained control of his facial muscles. "Covering what?"

"The water rights. You can't have them. I'll be a mother to your son, and you can have the ranch and everything else, but you can't have the water rights." For a moment she thought she glimpsed icy rage in his brown eyes, but then he partially lowered his lids, effectively hiding his thoughts.

"What do you intend to do with them?" His voice was calm.

"Put them in a trust fund for my mother. Chick Gannen should have taken care of her, but he didn't, and neither did his father. This way, no matter what happens, she'll always be provided for."

Sitting up straight, Matthew picked up his hat and circled the brim with a finger. Around and around. Finally he said simply, "No." Slowly he rose to his feet. "No marriage, no happy bridegroom, no prenuptial agreement."

Charlotte felt the blood drain from her head. She clutched the back of the nearest chair, an old wooden rocker. "I see." His only reason for marrying her was to obtain the water rights. "That certainly clarifies the situation, doesn't it?"

"It did for me." He halted beside her. "I doubt if it clears anything up for you. You're so blinded by resentment and hatred for Charlie and Chick Gannen, you can't see the nose on your own freckled face."

"How I feel about them has nothing—"

"It has everything," he said curtly. "You've painted them as villains, you hate them, and you think because Charlie and Chick and I come from the same place, the same background, we're cut from the same mold. The only reason you want to put those water rights in a trust for your mom is you don't trust me. You can't get it through your thick redheaded skull I am not Charlie or Chick Gannen." He walked deliberately to the front door, clapped his hat on his head and turned to face her. "Adios, cream puff." He reached for the doorknob, hesitated, tossed his hat to the floor and swiftly retraced his steps to her side. "This is for the stock pond," he muttered harshly, his mouth claiming hers.

For a moment Charlotte stood frozen, one hand still glued to the back of the rocker. Then, with a small whimper, she wound her arms around Matthew's neck and returned his kiss. If the kiss was started in revenge, it quickly transformed into passion. While Matthew's hands possessively roamed her body, his mouth laid claim to her lowered eyelids, her cheekbones, her jaw, her ears, her forehead and, of course, her mouth. She gasped as his fingers found her swollen breast and teased the hard, aching tip. He instantly took advantage of her parted lips. His kiss was deep and thorough and totally shattering. When Matthew finally lifted his head, Charlotte groped blindly for the rocker, clinging desperately to it with shaking hands.

Reaching in his pocket, Matthew pulled out a bundle of envelopes. "I almost forgot. Letters from Chick to Charlie from Vietnam. The last one must have come after

Chick died, because Charlie never opened it. Mom found them yesterday while she was cleaning some drawers." At the door Matthew swept up his hat. "I'm staying down the street." He named a nearby hotel. "Since Tim's asleep, I'll pick him up in the morning." The door closed silently behind him.

Charlotte staggered around the rocking chair and fell into it with a thud. The envelopes dropped to her lap. Matthew Thorneton was nothing but a rude, over-bearing, long-legged cowboy. She ran a finger over her lips. Skin against skin. That's all it was when his lips touched hers. Skin against skin.

Aunt Faye walked into the living room from the kitchen. "The way you've been acting since you returned from the ranch, I suspected something was going on."

"How long you been listening?" Charlotte asked dully.

"I didn't intend to eavesdrop. I had indigestion and came down for some medicine. When I heard you and Matt in here I thought I could tiptoe in and out without disturbing you, but then he started to leave, so I thought I'd better wait."

"And you saw the kiss and think you know what's going on."

"Saw the kiss, heard some of what he said and know exactly what's going on." Aunt Faye sat down on the sofa, folded her arms across her chest and looked steadily at Charlotte. "Do you?"

Charlotte leaned her head wearily against the wooden rungs of the rocker. "If nothing else, this experience has taught me how Mom came to grief over Chick Gannen." She shuffled the envelopes in her lap. "It's a very powerful thing, isn't it?"

"What is?"

"This magic elixir Western men have." Charlotte set the rocker into motion. "It's a myth, you know, that cowboys are strong and tall and brave and true. Cowboys are highly overrated as the ultimate specimens of mankind. I prefer men in spotless, immaculately creased tuxedos to rugged macho males in dusty jeans and muddy boots."

Aunt Faye sighed. "Lying to me is bad enough. But lying to yourself..."

The rocker creaked in the quiet room. "I didn't want to fall in love with him. He's arrogant, single-minded and a cowboy. I didn't fall in love with a man, I fell in love with an icon. Like mother, like daughter." She rocked steadily. "He can be gentle and considerate. He's kind to animals and good to his mother, and if you could see him with Tim..." She rocked harder. "Do you suppose I've been looking for a father figure? Except—" she abruptly halted the rocker "—he's so darned sexy."

"It sounds to me," Aunt Faye said slowly, "like all this cowboy nonsense is a smoke screen. What are you really afraid of?"

Charlotte gave her aunt a tremulous smile. "I never could fool you, could I?" She crumpled the envelopes in her lap. "He's still in love with his dead wife. What am I going to do?"

What was the point of having an aunt if she made you solve your own problems? Charlotte thought, not for the first time, as she crossed the carpeted lobby. The clerk referred her to a nearby bank of house phones. Taking a deep breath, Charlotte picked up the receiver and asked for Matthew's room. The ringing seemed to go on forever before the hotel switchboard operator asked if she'd like to leave a message. Charlotte declined. It was too late. He'd gone. She should have considered how early Matthew arose. They'd probably passed on the street.

"What are you doing here?"

Charlotte froze before turning slowly to face the owner of the low, growling voice. "How did you know it was me?"

One swift glance took in her simple peach-colored silk trouser outfit. "I recognized the back of your head."

She ventured a smile. "By the red hair or the thick skull?"

"That remains to be seen." His fingers closed around her arm, and he led her to the elevator.

Inside the cage, Charlotte stared at the numbers clicking off above the door. What if this was a big mistake? How had her mother at age twenty been so sure of Chick Gannen?

The elevator doors slid open. Down the hall, Matthew unlocked a door and ushered her inside. "I assume you're here to see me."

"Yes." Warm moist air from Matthew's shower hung in the room. Ignoring the rumpled bed, Charlotte walked to the window and feigned interest in the view. Her palms were sweaty; her heart hammered in triple time. Sensing Matthew behind her, she took a deep breath and turned. "I guess you could say I'm here about the water rights."

Matthew stuck his hands in his pockets, studying her through narrowed eyes. "I thought the offer I made for buying everything was reasonable, but I take it you want more."

She was going about this all wrong. She tried again. "Last night you said you wouldn't marry me because I didn't trust you. Suppose I were to tell you the water rights would be the bride's gift to the groom?" Her words were met with a charged silence.

After several long moments, Matthew said abruptly, "The letters from Chick. I suppose he wrote Charlie about your mother and his plans to marry her."

The cold anger in his eyes stunned her. "I don't see—"

"Obviously," Matthew snapped. "You just can't separate me from your father or your grandfather, can you? Chick wasn't as bad as you thought, therefore, neither am I." He strode to the door and yanked it open. "End of conversation."

Charlotte moved in a daze across the room. Matters had gone awry, and she wasn't sure...the letters. She stopped in front of Matthew. "Do you think the only reason I'm willing to trust you is because of something I read in Chick Gannen's letters?"

"Not Chick Gannen," he snarled. "Your father. Say it. Chick Gannen was your father." He crossed to the window, his back rigid. "Say it and then get out." He flung the words over his shoulder.

Charlotte pushed the door shut, backing against it. "Chick Gannen was my biological father. I've always known that, but I wanted a real father, the kind of father you are to Tim."

"I can't help you with that."

On either side of her thighs her splayed fingers pressed against the metal door. "You were right last night. I hated them both for not giving me what I wanted so badly. I told myself if they knew me, they'd have loved me and wanted me."

Without turning, Matthew said, "They would have."

At least he was listening. "Maybe. I didn't want to go to the ranch. As long as I didn't know for sure, I could tell myself anything I wanted. Now, I don't know. My thinking is all muddled. What Charles Gannen did to my mother was unforgivable, but maybe he wasn't all bad. As for Chick—'' she hesitated ''—as for my father, my mother loved him. She never had doubts. I should have trusted her feelings.''

''Because Chick told Charlie he wanted to marry your mother?''

''I haven't read the letters. I will because I can't give them to Mom unless I know there's nothing in them to hurt her, but last night—'' she swallowed hard ''—I had other things on my mind.'' It was now or never. She plunged ahead. ''I was wondering if I'd fit into that wedding dress your mom was unpacking, and wondering what kind of mother I'd make Tim and any strawberry-blond babies.''

Matthew slowly turned. ''Tim would be happy with any woman who likes rats and who would save him from having Paula as a stepmother.''

He couldn't have misunderstood she was saying she'd marry him, but he was hardly rushing to her side. She knew why. Lara. The metal door was cold against her spine. Cold for courage, she told herself. ''I know you'll always love Lara. In a way you're lucky. I'm probably the one person in the world who understands how some people are able to give their heart only once. I mean, look at my mother. After Chick, my father, there was never anyone else for her. I understand you can't love me.'' Matthew was backlit by the window, his face in shadow. ''Honestly I do, so I won't be making demands, at least that kind, on you. And Tim needs a mother, and I'm not the one you'd pick, but it could work.'' His watchful stillness and continued silence spurred her nervously into further speech. ''And the kissing's OK. You seem to enjoy that so I don't think we'll have trouble there. You said Tim wants a little baby and I wouldn't mind. If you don't. People have satis-

factory, uh, bedroom lives even if they're not in love.''
She ran out of words, defeated by his lack of response.

Matthew stirred. "After Lara died, I knew the bullet
that robbed her of life also robbed me of the ability to
love other women. And that was fine with me. I knew
I could never endure that kind of pain again. Then I
came to Denver and saw you. I disliked you on sight."

Intense pain slashed through her.

"You looked soft and frivolous and about as necessary
and use useful as a prom dress on a milk cow," he said
quietly, resting a hip on the windowsill and crossing his
booted feet at the ankles. "And I wanted, with an in-
tensity I've never ever known, to have you in my bed."

The astonishing words spoken in such a casual voice
rendered Charlotte speechless.

"You were so full of hate for Charlie, and so damned
stubborn, I expect the sexual attraction you held for me
would have quickly evaporated. Then I saw the way you
yielded to your mother's wishes, and it was crystal clear
I was the only one in the room surprised by your will-
ingness to sacrifice for her. Which meant there was more
to you than I thought, making you more dangerous."
He uttered a hard laugh. "I was caught between a rock
and a hard spot. I wanted the ranch and the water, but
I sure as hell didn't want you around complicating my
life. You owe me for a lot of sleepless nights, cream
puff."

She felt faint. Matthew was trying to explain why he
wouldn't marry her. "Never mind." She fumbled for
the doorknob.

"I convinced myself I'd imagined my reaction to you.
Even believed it until you walked through the door at
the airport. I felt like a horse had kicked me in the
stomach. I figured my choices were a quick affair or
keep out of your way. I should have known no red-

headed granddaughter of Charlie's would cooperate. The one thing I did know was that I'd already had one wife decide ranch living wasn't exciting and glamorous enough for her. I sure as hell never considered you for my wife."

"And Tim forced your hand. I'm sorry." Mortified by the scalding tears blurring her vision, she finally found the doorknob and tugged furiously, but the door refused to budge.

"The day you dumped me in the stock pond I swore to myself I was either going to marry you or strangle you." Matthew stood in front of her, an outstretched arm holding the door firmly shut. "I decided to marry you."

"Very funny!" All Charlotte wanted was to escape. Dodging his attempt to kiss her, she said, "I haven't forgotten you're planning to marry Paula."

"I'm not marrying Paula." He brushed a thumb lightly across her cheek. "How could I when all I think about is a certain redhead?" He smiled at her, his eyes gleaming with a sensuous warmth.

Charlotte's insides erupted into chaos. Concentrating on the pulse beating at the base of his throat, she breathlessly reminded him, "Paula told Tim you were marrying her. Your mom was unpacking a wedding dress for her."

"Mom's been digging into drawers and pulling out junk all week. When Tim and I had our conversation, I thought he was asking about you. As for Paula, she's always been a liar." He maneuvered her body between his hard strength and the door. "She's Lara's sister, but she has no claim on my heart."

"I know." Matthew's hips scalded hers; the rise and fall of his s chest as he breathed brushed the sensitive tips of her breasts. Her heart pounded. "You still love Lara." The pain hurt more than she thought it would.

Matthew tipped her face to meet his gaze, his hands encircled her neck. "I can't change my past even if I wanted to. Lara and I shared a wonderful love, which was blessed and enriched by Tim. But the man who loved her is no longer who I am. Lara was my past." He slid his palms along her shoulders. "My present and future is a redheaded lady who's kind to small boys and rats, loyal to her family and pugnacious in their defense. She's determined and courageous."

She still dared not hope. "This isn't because of what you think I did for your mother?" she asked slowly.

Matthew's response was instantaneous, his fingers digging convulsively into her arms. "When I saw you standing on the road, covered with mud, your clothes torn...I was so damned scared and so grateful you were OK." He cleared the hoarseness from his throat. "It wasn't marriage I had on my mind then, believe me. Realizing I might have lost you filled me with such overwhelming hunger and need, I wanted to strip you naked and make you mine right there in the mud."

Charlotte felt light-headed; her blood surged through her veins. "I couldn't have gotten any muddier."

He planted a kiss on her nose. "I was working out how to court you when Tim jumped the gun."

Happiness made her giddy. "The most romantic moment of my life. 'Why don't you marry Charlotte, Dad?'" she mimicked, making a face at him before pitching her voice lower. "'Sure. Why not? What do you think, Charlotte?'"

Matthew grinned. "I suppose it did lack a certain something. Not that your proposals were much better. First, refusing to trust me, hardly the act of a woman in love. Then, babbling about how understanding you'd be." The grin faded away. "I know living on a ranch and sleeping with a cowboy have never been your dream, but will you marry me and allow me to love you forever?'' His kiss was gentle yet demanding, possessive yet generous, full of exotic promises and familiar pleasures.

When at last he raised his head, Charlotte felt flushed from head to toe. ''I was so foolishly determined not to fall in love with you, I didn't even realize I had.''

''I had no intention of letting you get away.'' Matthew wove his fingers deep into her tousled hair. ''Buying Charlie's ranch was going to be the most prolonged business transaction you'd ever been involved in. I figured you'd marry me just to get away from the paperwork.'' He gave her a mock scowl. ''I may even forgive you for that damned impertinent prenuptial agreement nonsense.''

The trouble with cowboys, Charlotte thought, was they tended to be irritatingly smug and arrogant. She trailed a finger along his rock-solid jaw. ''I've changed my mind about that.''

''I should think so.''

''I've changed it back. I want a prenuptial agreement.''

''Damn it, cream puff, you—''

Charlotte touched a finger to his lips. ''First of all, I'll expect you to use my name. Charlotte, not cream puff.''

Golden flames leaped in Matthew's eyes. ''I see.'' He nibbled along the edge of her finger. ''What else?''

''You won't call me prissy.''

''Won't I?'' Having nibbled his way to her wrist, he was busy planting kisses there.

''You're to agree my hair is strawberry-blond, not red.''

''Mmm.'' He moved his attentions to her neck.

''And you have to promise,'' she said desperately as Matthew painstakingly slid one button after another through narrow slits, "you'll never buy me a flannel nightgown."

"I solemnly promise, cream puff—" he dropped her silk blouse to the floor "—I will never, ever—" a wisp of peach-colored lace followed the blouse "—buy you a flannel nightgown." With agonizingly slow deliberation he slid his hands to her waist. "I've been waiting a long time to find out just how far down freckles dare go on a certain redhaired lady."

Later he even agreed the way she'd said his name wasn't the least bit prissy.

Take 4 bestselling love stories FREE

Plus get a FREE surprise gift!

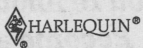

HARLEQUIN®

Don't miss these Harlequin favorites by some of our most distinguished authors!
And now you can receive a discount by ordering two or more titles!

HT#25593	WHAT MIGHT HAVE BEEN by Glenda Sanders	$2.99 U.S. ☐ /$3.50 CAN.	☐
HP#11713	AN UNSUITABLE WIFE by Lindsay Armstrong	$2.99 U.S. ☐ /$3.50 CAN.	☐
HR#03356	BACHELOR'S FAMILY by Jessica Steele	$2.99 U.S.☐ /$3.50 CAN.	☐
HS#70494	THE BIG SECRET by Janice Kaiser	$3.39	☐
HI#22196	CHILD'S PLAY by Bethany Campbell	$2.89	☐
HAR#16553	THE MARRYING TYPE by Judith Arnold	$3.50 U.S. ☐ /$3.99 CAN.	☐
HH#28844	THE TEMPTING OF JULIA by Maura Seger	$3.99 U.S ☐ /$4.50 CAN.	☐

(limited quantities available on certain titles)

AMOUNT	$
DEDUCT: 10% DISCOUNT FOR 2+ BOOKS	$
POSTAGE & HANDLING ($1.00 for one book, 50¢ for each additional)	$
APPLICABLE TAXES*	$_____
TOTAL PAYABLE	$_____
(check or money order—please do not send cash)	

To order, complete this form and send it, along with a check or money order for the total above, payable to Harlequin Books, to: **In the U.S.:** 3010 Walden Avenue, P.O. Box 9047, Buffalo, NY 14269-9047; **In Canada:** P.O. Box 613, Fort Erie, Ontario, L2A 5X3.

Name: _____

Address:_____ City: _____

State/Prov.: _____ Zip/Postal Code: _____

*New York residents remit applicable sales taxes.
 Canadian residents remit applicable GST and provincial taxes.

HBACK-OD2

You're About to Become a *Privileged Woman*

Reap the rewards of fabulous free gifts and benefits with proofs-of-purchase from Harlequin and Silhouette books

Pages & Privileges™

It's our way of thanking you for buying our books at your favorite retail stores.

Harlequin and Silhouette— the most privileged readers in the world!

For more information about Harlequin and Silhouette's PAGES & PRIVILEGES program call the Pages & Privileges Benefits Desk: 1-503-794-2499

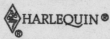

HARLEQUIN ®

HR-PP77